LOVE FOR SALE

There were tears on her cheeks and her eyelashes were wet, and he thought as he looked down at her that she was lovelier in her distress than anyone he had ever seen.

"I promise you need no longer be afraid," he said.

As she continued to stare at him with her lips parted, he bent towards her and his mouth was on hers.

For a moment she could not believe it was happening.

Then as she felt his lips take possession of her, Udela knew that she loved him, and this was why she had been so frantically afraid of losing him.

For a moment Udela was hardly aware of what she was doing.

She could only think of the wonder of the Duke's lips and that he had kissed her was the most marvellous, perfect thing that had ever happened.

Bantam Books by Barbara Cartland
Ask your bookseller for the titles you have missed

97 THE GHOST WHO FELL
      IN LOVE
98 THE DRUMS OF LOVE
99 ALONE IN PARIS
100 THE PRINCE AND THE
      PEKINGESE
101 THE SERPENT OF SATAN
102 THE TREASURE IS LOVE
103 LIGHT OF THE MOON
104 THE PRISONER OF LOVE
108 LOVE CLIMBS IN
109 A NIGHTINGALE SANG
110 TERROR IN THE SUN
115 WOMEN HAVE HEARTS
117 LOVE IN THE CLOUDS

118 THE POWER AND THE
      PRINCE
120 FREE FROM FEAR
121 LITTLE WHITE DOVES OF
      LOVE
122 THE PERFECTION OF
      LOVE
123 BRIDE TO THE KING
124 PUNISHED WITH LOVE
125 THE DAWN OF LOVE
126 LUCIFER AND THE ANGEL
127 OLA AND THE SEA WOLF
128 THE PRUDE AND THE
      PRODIGAL
129 LOVE FOR SALE

Barbara Cartland's Library of Love Series

THE MONEY MOON
ONLY A GIRL'S LOVE
THE BRIDGE OF KISSES
SON OF THE TURK

Books of Love and Revelation

THE TREASURE OF HO

Other books by Barbara Cartland

I SEEK THE MIRACULOUS

LOVE FOR SALE

Barbara Cartland

BANTAM BOOKS · TORONTO · NEW YORK · LONDON

LOVE FOR SALE
A Bantam Book

PRINTING HISTORY
E.P. Dutton edition published July 1980
A Selection of Doubleday Book Club October 1980
Bantam edition / November 1980

All rights reserved.
Copyright © 1980 by Barbara Cartland.
This book may not be reproduced in whole or in part, by
mimeograph or any other means, without permission.
For information address: Bantam Books, Inc.

ISBN 0-553-13984-3

Published simultaneously in the United States and Canada

Bantam Books are published by Bantam Books, Inc. Its trade-
mark, consisting of the words "Bantam Books" and the por-
trayal of a bantam, is Registered in U.S. Patent and Trademark
Office and in other countries. Marca Registrada. Bantam
Books, Inc., 666 Fifth Avenue, New York, New York 10103.

PRINTED IN THE UNITED STATES OF AMERICA

0 9 8 7 6 5 4 3 2 1

Author's Note

The keepers of the bawdy-houses in the eighteenth and nineteenth centuries made great fortunes. Some imported their women from the Continent, but most of them enticed decent girls into their clutches and then there was no escape. Servant-girls coming to London from the country were easy prey and were offered lifts to their places of employment in comfortable carriages, or were tempted by offers of more money.

No young girl was really safe in the streets of London until after the First World War, and the history of the period contains heart-rending stories of the manner in which they were mistreated and their early deaths from drink, drugs, and disease.

Chapter One
1820

As the Duke of Oswestry drew up his Phaeton outside the house in Park Street, he wished that he could drive on.

He was calling on Lady Marlene Kelston only because he had received not one but three letters from her in the last twenty-four hours, each one telling him more voluably than the last that she must see him immediately.

He could not imagine what had occurred to make her write to him after they had been parted for nearly three months.

He had had a brief and fiery love-affair with the Lady Marlene, and when it had ended in an acrimonious quarrel in which they had been extremely offensive to each other, he told himself he had been a fool in the first place to become involved with her.

Lady Marlene, who had been the toast of St. James's for the last two years, was a very determined woman.

The Duke's mother had always said warningly: "There is bad blood in the Kelstons."

The Duke acknowledged that she had been

right, after he had become intimate with Lady Marlene and found out that the bad blood did indeed reveal itself in her character.

To the world she was glamorous with an unmistakable allure, and her impetuous disregard for the social conventions had a charm of its own.

She had been married while the Duke was fighting with Wellington's Army, and her husband had been wounded at Waterloo and had finally died of his injuries three years ago.

Hardly allowing the conventional time of mourning to pass, Lady Marlene had appeared like a meteor on the Social World and there had been no doubt as to her success.

She was in fact extremely beautiful, and when finally the Duke succumbed to her pursuit of him, he knew it was inevitable.

What he had not expected, nor in fact had anyone else, was that Lady Marlene's tantrums and insatiable demands would bore him so quickly.

But then, if Lady Marlene was unpredictable, so was the Duke.

He was nearly at his thirtieth birthday and had a vast experience of women of all sorts.

He had been chased, pursued, and stalked since the moment he had left School, for there was no one in the whole country who was more eligible as a matrimonial *parti* and no man who was as handsome and irresistible to the opposite sex.

He was also extremely elusive, but it was his fastidiousness and his desire for perfection which made him find that women palled on him so quickly that the Regent had said jokingly:

"Your conquests last such a short time, Oswestry, that we shall soon find ourselves, now that the war is over, having to import females from the Continent for your delectation."

The Duke had laughed dutifully. At the same time, there was a darkness in his eyes which the Regent did not notice.

The one thing he really disliked was talking about his love-affairs and he thought ingenuously that his private life should be private.

But in the *Beau Monde,* where every tit-bit of scandal was collected and mouthed over until there was nothing left to say, it was impossible for anyone as important or as attractive as the Duke to keep anything private.

This was another reason why he had finished with Lady Marlene. She talked, and in his eyes that was unforgivable.

Handing the reins of his superb horses over to his groom, he stepped down from the Phaeton, noting as he did so that the crested buttons on the uniform of the lackey who was waiting at the open front door needed cleaning.

On her husband's death Lady Marlene had reverted to her family name, wishing, she announced in a somewhat aggressive manner, "to wipe out the past, and that includes my late and unlamented husband!"

The Dowagers who had always disapproved of her agreed that this was the heartless as well as outrageous manner in which one would expect her to behave.

However, they had been aware since the war ended that Lady Marlene had no use for a man who was crippled, even though his injuries were received in performing a deed of conspicuous gallantry on the battlefield.

"For me, a man must be a man," Lady Marlene had said when somebody had rebuked her for disparaging her husband, and there was no doubt, on this occasion at any rate, that she was speaking the truth.

"What on earth does she want with me?" the Duke asked himself as he was shown across the marble Hall and a footman opened the door of a Salon on the other side of it.

The Duke knew the house well. He had called often enough when he and Lady Marlene were enamoured of each other.

It had always struck him that it was badly decorated and that the furniture needed polishing.

It was actually the family house of the Kelstons and was owned by Lady Marlene's brother, the Earl of Stanwick.

As he seldom came to London, it would have been absurd for her to set up house on her own, besides being very much more expensive.

The Kelstons never had enough money, which was not surprising as they were all as extravagant as Lady Marlene, but, as her bills were invariably paid by her admirers, she was in a better position than the rest of her relatives.

The Salon was empty and the footman murmured: "I'll tell Her Ladyship that you are here, Your Grace," and shut the door.

The Duke walked slowly towards the mantelpiece, still worrying as to what Lady Marlene had to tell him.

His impulse on receiving her first note was to ignore it, but when the second and third arrived he had the uncomfortable feeling that if he did not go to her, she would come to him.

This was something she had done more than once in the past, turning up at Oswestry House in Berkeley Square without an invitation and involving him in uncomfortable situations with his older and more staid relations who disapproved of her and were prepared to say so, even though they knew it annoyed the Duke.

However, they did not say as much as they might have done, for the simple reason that they were rather frightened of him.

He took his position as head of the family seriously, and from the moment he inherited, he was very much more circumspect in everything he did in public than he had been when his father was alive.

"You are getting old and staid!" Lady Marlene had often taunted him.

This was usually when he would not take part in one of her more outrageous escapades or had refused categorically to accompany her to some Ball or party given by people of whom he did not approve.

He remembered now how fierce their quarrels had been, often as fiery and tempestuous as their love-making, and he told himself that as far as he was concerned, he was very glad it was over.

The door opened and Lady Marlene came in.

There was no doubt that she was beautiful, even the Duke had to acknowledge that.

The lights in her red hair flickered like flames on her head, and her eyes, which were unmistakably green, glinted beneath their dark lashes.

She walked towards him and there was an expression on her face to which he could not put a name.

Then as she reached him she said:

"So you have come at last!"

"I cannot imagine why you wished to see me."

"It is important, Randolph."

"So I gather."

Lady Marlene tilted her head a little to one side

as she looked at him. It was a characteristic movement which her admirers found enchanting.

"You are exceedingly handsome," she said,
"perhaps better-looking than any other man I have
ever known. I cannot imagine why we quarrelled
with each other."

"I cannot believe you brought me here to listen
to compliments," the Duke answered coldy. "Tell
me what you want, Marlene. I am driving two
young horses and they will be fidgeting."

"Horses! Always horses!" she exclaimed with a
sharp note in her voice. "I always swore they
meant more to you than any woman."

The Duke did not reply. He only waited and
she knew he was impatient. He found it extremely
irritating when a woman did not come to the point.

"I sent for you," Lady Marlene said after a little pause, "to tell you that I am having a baby!"

Just for a moment the Duke was still. Then he
said:

"Why should you imagine that would interest
me? Obviously the person who should be informed
is Charles Nazeby."

"He knows!" Lady Marlene said briefly. "But,
as you are well aware, Charles is penniless."

The Duke's lips curved slightly in a cynical smile.

"You can hardly expect me to pay for Nazeby's indiscretions?"

"I am not asking for money."

"Then what?"

"Marriage!"

If she had exploded a bomb in front of him, the
Duke could not have been more astonished.

He stared at her in amazement. Then he said:

"Can I really credit that you are asking me to
marry you because you are expecting Nazeby's
child?"

"It might be yours."

"But you know as well as I do that it is nothing of the sort!"

"I think I should be the person to choose who should father my unwanted brat," Lady Marlene said, "and who could give him a better start in life than a Duke?"

There was a momentary silence before the Duke replied:

"If that is all you have to say to me, Marlene, I have wasted my time in coming here, so I will bid you good-day."

As he spoke, he made a movement as if he would walk towards the door, but she was standing in front of him and now she said, with her eyes searching his:

"It is no use running away, Randolph. I always intended to marry you before we had that foolish and unnecessary quarrel, and I shall, if nothing else, make you an amusing wife."

"You may intend to marry me," the Duke replied, "but I have no intention of marrying you, or for that matter anyone else!"

"That was always your attitude!" Lady Marlene retorted. "But you know that you will have to marry sometime, rather than let Julius inherit, and this is the moment to disappoint him once and for all!"

"Before we become embroiled any further in this conversation," the Duke said, "let me make it clear that I will not marry you and there is no point in discussing it."

"There is every point," Lady Marlene contradicted, "because if I have to marry someone, I prefer it to be you."

"I suppose I must take that as a compliment,

but unfortunately you expressed your true feelings for me very forcefully when we parted."

"How can you be so tiresome as to remember what we said when we both lost our tempers and were only trying to hurt each other? Whatever I may have said, I loved you, Randolph, and I love you now."

"Very touching!" the Duke said sarcastically. "But I cannot believe that Nazeby will be very pleased."

"Charles has nothing to do with it! He cannot support me, and anyway he has already suggested that it might easily be your child rather than his."

"That does not surprise me," the Duke said. "Nazeby never would face up to his responsibilities."

"But you always do, and therefore, Randolph, the sooner we are married the better!"

The Duke sighed.

"I thought I had made it clear that I will not marry you and that I disclaim all responsibility for any child you may bear. Great Heavens, it is three months since we last saw each other!"

"Not quite three months, so it could possibly be yours."

"Only a fool would believe that, and I am not a fool, Marlene!"

Again the Duke took a step towards the door, and again Lady Marlene was in front of him.

Now her green eyes narrowed and there was a touch of venom in her voice as she said:

"Do you really intend to do nothing for me?"

"Nothing!"

"Very well then. I shall immediately send for my brother. He will not only believe me, but he will support me in making you see sense."

The Duke was quite certain that the Earl of

Stanwick would be quick to realise the advantages of having a rich and Ducal brother-in-law.

He was a fiery man, as wild and unpredictable as his sister, and even more dangerous.

He had been involved in innumerable duels, fights, and even riots.

He caused trouble wherever he went, and after the last of his periodical visits to London, his friends as well as his enemies, when he left, heaved a sigh of relief.

The Duke was well aware what trouble the Earl could cause, and although he was not in the least afraid of duelling with him, he knew that it would result in a scandal which would be reported in the newspapers.

Every detail of their quarrel over Lady Marlene would be known not only to the *Beau Monde* but to the ordinary public.

This was something he disliked above all else, and he felt every instinct within him shrink from the gossip which would ensue.

As if she knew what he was thinking, Lady Marlene said with a note of triumph in her voice:

"Hector will believe me, and Hector will make certain, Randolph, that you do not leave me to bear the consequences of our love alone."

The Duke did not reply and after a moment she said:

"It is much better to give in without all the fuss; you will have to do so in the end."

"If there is one thing I really abhor," the Duke said, and his voice was icy, "it is being black-mailed!"

Lady Marlene threw back her head and laughed.

"If that word is supposed to intimidate me, it does nothing of the sort. Very well, Randolph, I am blackmailing you, and I am quite certain that when I tell my relations how despicably you are behaving, they will be prepared to blackmail you too!"

Her eyes were on his face, looking for some reaction, but the Duke's expression, although grim, did not change, and she did not have the satisfaction of realising how much she was perturbing him.

"Now let me see . . . " she went on, "my Aunt Agnes is hereditary Lady-of-the-Bedchamber to Her Majesty. I am sure the Queen would be very upset at your behaviour, and my Uncle George is still, although he is over seventy-five, a Lord-in-Waiting. They can spread the word round Buckingham Palace."

She was aware as she spoke that the Duke was looking at her and his eyes were like agates.

He was thinking that it was his own fault that he was now in this unpleasant and indeed dangerous situation.

How could he have guessed, how could he have known, that beneath that beautiful exterior there was the tongue and heart of a viper?

At this moment he felt a positive revulsion towards Marlene and he thought it was an aspersion on his own good taste that he should ever at any time have found her attractive.

With a sudden change of mood Lady Marlene said:

"Forgive me, Randolph, I did not mean to plague you. When you marry me I will behave with some propriety and we shall enjoy ourselves as we did before we fought in that stupid manner."

She paused as if she expected him to say something, but as he was silent she went on:

"You know I shall grace the Oswestry diamonds and give parties to which everybody will fight to be invited."

She smiled and it made her face even more beautiful than it was already.

"Think what fun it will be to put your odious brother's nose out of joint! I suppose you know that while he is not pestering you at the moment for money, he is behaving in a manner which would make your ancestors turn in their graves?"

"I have no wish to discuss with you anything that concerns Julius," the Duke said sharply. "What my brother does nor does not do is not your business, nor are you mine."

Now he moved past Lady Marlene before she could stop him and walked firmly towards the door.

"If that is your last word," she said, "I shall send for Hector."

"Send for him, and be damned!"

As the Duke said the last words he left the Salon, and Lady Marlene heard his footsteps moving across the marble Hall.

For a moment there was an expression of concern in her green eyes, then she smiled confidently.

"He will not escape this time . . . " she said aloud.

* * *

Driving back from his Club in his closed Brougham, the Duke was wondering, as he had wondered all the evening, what he should do.

Because he was so disturbed after his interview with Lady Marlene, he had sent a message excusing himself from the dinner-party he was supposed to have attended at Holland House and had gone instead to dine at White's Club.

There had been numerous friends there to welcome him, but they had found him surprisingly quiet and absent-minded, until at least three of them had asked:

"What is the matter with you, Randolph? You seem depressed."

The Duke had wanted to tell them that indeed he was depressed, but instead he merely admitted to a headache, and continued to worry.

He disliked the thought of a scandal, but he disliked even more the idea of marrying Marlene.

All the time when they had been physically attracted to each other he had always known that she was unstable and could, if anyone offended her, be vitriolic.

But he had never imagined for one moment that any woman would sink to the methods she was employing now, to force him to marry her, or would show herself in her true colours in a manner which left him disgusted and in fact apprehensive.

How could he contemplate accepting as a wife a virago, a woman with so few morals that she was prepared to foist on him another man's child—a man for whom in fact the Duke had no liking and less respect?

Sir Charles Nazeby was a waster, a man who lived on his wits and who, the Duke suspected, although he had no evidence to substantiate it, was not above cheating at cards.

That any child of his, if it was a boy, would one day become the Duke of Oswestry was a possibility which the Duke was determined to oppose, whatever the cost.

He was, although he never spoke of it, exceedingly proud that his family all through history had served the Monarchy and the country to the best of their abilities.

The family name was Westry and there had

been Westrys who had been great Statesmen, Westrys who had been extremely gallant on the field of battle, and Westrys who had sailed away to explore the world.

They had always commanded the respect and admiration of their contemporaries, and the Duke was determined that he would not defame their memory.

He thought now that he should have married and bred a son before he became involved with Lady Marlene, but he had wanted his marriage to be different.

Because he knew how many of his personal friends were unhappy or at least bored with the wives who had been chosen for them by their parents, he had fought to remain single.

He told anyone who urged him to walk up the aisle that he had decided to remain a bachelor.

He had always thought to himself that there was plenty of time to do later what was obviously his duty, when he no longer enjoyed his freedom as much as he did now.

It was not only that he liked running his houses and his vast possessions without any interference from a woman, but he was also honest enough to admit that he enjoyed being able to pick and choose from among the beautiful women who offered him their favours only too eagerly.

He was not particularly conceited, but he was well aware that every beauty in the *Beau Monde* considered it a feather in her cap if he became her lover.

It was pleasant to know that, unlike Lady Marlene, the majority of them remained friends and were exceedingly fond of him after their liaison was over.

Many, it was true, had broken hearts, or so

they averred, but the Duke thought cynically that few hearts were permanently damaged by love, and the wounds, if there were any, soon healed.

But now, out of the blue when he least expected it, Marlene Kelston was menacing him in a way he had never been menaced before.

Because everything about the situation was intolerable, he had suddenly risen from the card-table and without making any explanation had left the Club.

He did not even hear his friends call after him:

"Randolph, you have forgotten your winnings!"

Only after he had gone without replying did they look at one another and ask:

"What has happened to Oswestry? I have never known him to behave so strangely!"

"It must be a woman!" someone suggested.

There was laughter at this, and it was incredulous.

"A woman?" was the reply. "Have you ever known Oswestry to worry over a woman when he only has to lift his finger to have a hundred crowding round him?"

"That is true enough!" another man exclaimed. "And, dammit, with his looks and money, he ruins the market."

As the carriage drove down Berkeley Street and into Berkeley Square, the Duke felt as if he was turning a tread-mill round and round in his mind and never getting any further.

It was the same question which presented itself over and over again, and he could only find one answer—there was nothing he could do!

He was scowling in a manner which made the footman who opened the door of the carriage, as it drew up outside Oswestry House, look at him apprehensively.

His Grace was home early, which was unusual, and inevitably when something was wrong, the staff, most of whom had been with the Duke for many years, were aware of it.

Another footman had hurriedly run the red carpet across the pavement and the Butler was standing in the open doorway as the Duke stepped out.

The servants bowed their heads as he passed them. Then as he reached the two steps to the front door there was a sudden cry and a woman came running along the pavement to fling herself against the Duke, holding on to him and saying as she did so:

"Save ... me! Save ... me!"

She spoke frantically and the Duke turned towards her in surprise, to see a very young face looking up at him and two eyes dark with fear.

"Save me!" she cried again. "Help ... they are trying to ... catch me!"

The Butler moved hastily to the Duke's side and took the woman by the arm.

"That's quite enough of that!" he said. "Be off with you! We don't want any of your sort here!"

As he spoke, the stalwart young footman who had set down the carpet went to the other side of the woman.

"Leave this to us, Your Grace!" the Butler said.

As he spoke he pulled the woman backwards, and as if she realised that he intended to remove her, she gave another cry.

"Please ... please!" she cried. "I was ... told it was ... Lord Julius Westry's carriage ... but I am sure ... that was a lie!"

By this time the Butler and the footman had already dragged her several feet from the Duke and he moved onto the first step leading up to the front door.

Now he looked back to ask sharply:

"Who did you say?"

"Help me. . . please . . . help me!"

The woman was sobbing as she spoke.

"Leave her alone," the Duke ordered.

As the Butler and the footman took their hands from her arms, she ran forward again, her eyes misty with tears, and looked up at the Duke as she said:

"They . . . they are . . . trying to catch . . . me!"

The Duke looked to where in the darkness of the Square he could see two men standing irresolute, as if they had checked their pursuit of their victim when they saw to whom she was speaking.

"You mentioned a name just now," the Duke said. "Will you repeat it to me?"

"Lord . . . Julius . . . Westry . . . told me he had . . . employment for . . . me."

The Duke stared at her as if he wanted to be certain that she was speaking the truth. Then he said:

"Come into the house and you can tell me exactly what has happened to you."

The woman glanced over her shoulder, and, as if she too could see the men in the distance, she shuddered and moved quickly up the steps after the Duke, who had already reached the Hall.

He handed his evening-cloak, his high hat, and his cane to a footman, then walked across the marble floor.

She followed him, and as another footman opened a door they entered the Library.

It was a large, very impressive room with windows looking onto a garden at the back.

Now the curtains were closed and the light from

the candles showed books arranged in fine Chippendale cases, a large writing-table in the centre of the room under a painted ceiling, and a sofa and two wing-backed arm-chairs in front of a fireplace.

The Duke walked to stand with his back to the mantelshelf as he inspected his visitor.

He saw that she was small and very young and, he told himself with surprise, unexpectedly lovely.

She had very large eyes in a heart-shaped face, and her hair, under her plain, unfashionable bonnet, was the colour of ripening corn. Her eyes surprisingly were not blue but, unless he was mistaken, the grey of a wintry sea.

She was looking at him apprehensively and the terror was still in her expression and he saw that she was trembling.

"Come and sit down," he invited quietly.

As if his voice reassured her, she moved gracefully towards one of the wing-backed chairs and sat down on the edge of it, her hands in her lap.

He knew that her clothes were old-fashioned and, although in good taste, of inexpensive material.

He was sure, from what he had heard of her voice, that she was educated, and there was a refinement about her which told him she was of gentle birth.

He walked to the grog-tray which stood in a corner of the room.

"I think, as you have been through an unpleasant experience," he said, "that you need a drink. Would you prefer champagne or lemonade?"

"I ... I would like a ... glass of lemonade ... if you please."

As he poured it out, the Duke thought that it

was a choice he would never have offered to any of the women who usually sat in this room.

There was something so young about this girl that he had the feeling that she seldom if ever drank wine.

"Thank you . . . very much," she said as he handed her the glass.

As she took it, he realised that her hand was shaking, but he admired the way she was keeping control over herself.

As he thought he would seem less frightening, he sat down on a chair opposite her.

"Now tell me what has upset you," he asked, "and what Lord Julius Westry has to do with it."

The girl set her glass down on a table beside her chair and, clasping her hands together as she did so, answered:

"I feel that first . . . Sir . . . I should . . . apologise for imposing myself upon you . . . but I was so . . . frightened . . . and all I could think of was . . . trying to escape from the carriage which had met . . . me at the . . . Posting-Inn at Islington."

The Duke was aware that this was where the stage-coaches arrived from the North.

"I am glad that I was able to help you," he replied. "But you had better tell me exactly what happened, so that I can ensure you are not recaptured when you leave here—if that is what frightens you."

The girl drew in her breath and the Duke saw that once again she was terrified.

"D-do you . . . think they might . . . wait for me?"

"Who are they?"

"There were two men . . . one was on the b-box of the carriage . . . the other was . . . I think . . . a servant of the . . . h-house to which I was . . . taken."

"Which house was that?"

"I . . . I think it was . . . Number Twenty-seven Hay Hill."

The Duke started.

"Are you sure that is where you were going?"

"When Lord . . . Julius wrote to me, he said there would be a . . . carriage to meet me at Islington . . . but he did not say . . . where I was to go. It was only when I read the leaflet . . . that I guessed . . . and I was . . . very . . . very frightened!"

The Duke smiled.

"It sounds rather complicated," he said. "Suppose we start at the beginning and first you tell me your name."

"It is . . . Udela Hayward."

"And where do you live, Miss Hayward?"

"Just outside Huntingdon. My father was the Vicar of Little Storton."

"You say 'was.' Is he dead?"

Udela nodded.

"He . . . died three weeks ago."

There was a little sob in her voice, but she went on bravely:

"It was after he died that I . . . realised I had to . . . find employment of some sort. Then I met Lord Eldridge."

"How did you meet him?"

As she spoke, Udela could see so clearly the morning she had picked almost every flower that was in bloom in the Vicarage-garden to take to the cemetery.

Her father had loved flowers and she had thought that perhaps both he and her mother would look down from Heaven and see how well she had arranged the flowers on their graves.

The roses on her mother's favourite tree were

only in bud, but she picked them thinking that if
she put them in water, they would open and become a patch of the vivid pink which always reminded her of her mother.

It was the colour of happiness, Udela thought,
the happiness which had flown away when first her
mother had died, and now her father had left her
too.

She was walking from the Vicarage along the
dusty lane which led to the Church-yard when she
became aware of two riders coming towards her.

She noticed first their horses, because they were
particularly fine and her father had taught her to
appreciate the good points of a horse, and to ride
well, as he did himself.

Udela had never had the chance of riding the
type of horses she was seeing now, and only as
they drew level with her did she realise that one
of the riders was the young Squire, Lord Eldridge,
of whom her father had never approved.

However, she curtsyed politely and he drew his
horse to a standstill to say:

"Good-morning, Miss Hayward. I was sorry to
hear, when I returned home from London, that
your father had died."

"It was . . . very sudden . . . My Lord."

"My Agent informs me," Lord Eldridge went
on, "that I have to choose somebody to replace
him, but I will not force you to leave the Vicarage
until you are ready to do so."

"That is very . . . kind of Your Lordship. I
have been . . . wondering where I could go."

"You have relatives, I suppose?" Lord Eldridge
asked lightly.

He was a red-faced young man who had disappointed his father by being sent down from Oxford

and whose only ambition had appeared to be to spend his money on riotous living.

Once he had succeeded to the title, the parties that had taken place at Eldridge Park had all the village whispering in shocked tones, and Udela had thought it not surprising that the family pew remained empty Sunday after Sunday.

But now she felt that Lord Eldridge was being kind, and her voice was grateful as she answered:

"None, My Lord, but I will find ... somewhere I can go as soon as I have tidied up ... everything at the Vicarage."

"That is all right then."

Lord Eldridge would have ridden on, but his companion said:

"Introduce me, Edward. Perhaps I can help this pretty young lady."

Lord Eldridge looked at him in surprise, then he said:

"Miss Hayward—let me introduce Lord Julius Westry, who wishes to make your acquaintance."

Udela curtsyed again, and Lord Julius, to his friend's surprise, dismounted from his horse and, leading it by the bridle, walked to her side.

"I heard you say, Miss Hayward, that you have to find employment. Have you a place in mind?"

"No ... I have not, My Lord," Udela replied, "except perhaps to be a Governess ... I am very fond of children."

"You look rather young for a post of that sort," Lord Julius remarked. "How old are you?"

"I am eighteen, My Lord."

As she spoke, she looked at him and thought there was something about him she did not like.

He was tall and broad-shouldered, but his eyes were too close together and it gave his face, which otherwise might have been good-looking, a somewhat sinister expression.

"I think I might be able to help you," he was saying. "Do not commit yourself to any particular position until you hear from me."

His eyes seemed to flicker over her, taking in, she thought a little shyly, not only her face but her figure.

She was suddenly conscious that her cotton gown, which she had had for some years and had been washed a great many times, was rather tight, and because of the way Lord Julius was scrutinising her, she felt the colour rise in her cheeks.

"Thank . . . you, My Lord."

"Wait for my letter," he said, and it was a command.

Udela curtsyed to him, then again to Lord Eldridge.

Only as she hurried away with her flowers into the Church-yard was she conscious of a desire, which she could not explain, to run and keep on running.

*   *   *

As Lord Julius had told her to wait for his letter, she had not written, as she had intended, to a Domestic Bureau which she knew existed in Huntingdon.

She was not certain what she should say or in what capacity she should offer herself.

There were, as she knew only too well, only two types of employment open for a lady: that of Governess or of companion, and she had the uncomfortable feeling that Lord Julius was right when he said she was too young to be the former.

'I could look after very small children,' Udela thought.

As she stared at her reflection in the mirror she wished that she looked older and not so very young.

She was frightened of the future, but she would have been still more frightened if she had overheard what Lord Julius had said as, having mounted his horse, he rode away down the dusty lane.

"How could I expect, Edward," he said to Lord Eldridge, "to find such a beauty hidden here in your village?"

"She is rather pretty," Lord Eldridge admitted.

"Pretty!" Lord Julius exclaimed. "Dressed in style, and Mother Crawley knows how to dress them, she will be a sensation!"

"So that is what you have in mind!" Lord Eldridge exclaimed.

"But of course!" Lord Julius replied. "I am always on the look-out for suitable material, but it is not often that I hit the 'jack-pot' as I believe I have this morning!"

They rode on for a few minutes in silence. Then Lord Eldridge said:

"Poor little devil! I am sorry for her, but I suppose there is no alternative."

Chapter Two

Udela took a little sip of the lemonade, and as she set the glass down carefully on the table again, the Duke said:

"So you waited for a letter from Lord Julius. Surely it was rather strange for you to expect to be offered a position by a man you had met only once?"

Udela's eye-lashes flickered as if she was shy, and she replied in a low voice:

"To be honest, Sir, I expected that he would ... forget, and I did try to find a ... position locally."

"How did you do that?" the Duke asked.

"I learnt there was a lady in the next village who required a Governess for her two small sons. I went to see her."

"What happened?"

"She said she thought I was too young, and although it may sound presumptuous, I think she ... disliked my ... looks."

The Duke thought that was very likely. No

woman would wish to engage a Governess who looked as lovely as the girl opposite him.

"Then I presume Lord Julius's letter arrived?"

"Yes, Sir. I received it three days ago, and he told me to come to London on the coach that would arrive at the Two-Headed Swan at Islington at half-after-six. Unfortunately, there was an accident, and in consequence we did not arrive until very late; in fact I suppose it was just over half-an-hour ago."

"But the carriage was still waiting for you?"

"Lord Julius had said it would be there, and the moment the stage-coach arrived, the footman asked if I was Miss Hayward."

"And you still did not know where you were going?"

"No. Lord Julius said in the letter that he had an excellent position for me in which he was sure I would be very happy."

The Duke did not speak and Udela went on:

"I thought it was very . . . kind of him, and of course because he was a friend of the Squire he would know about me . . . and who my . . . parents had . . . been."

Her voice had faltered for a moment; then, with what the Duke thought was a commendable effort, she lifted her chin, as if she was determined to control her emotions.

"So you got into the carriage," he prompted. "But what happened to upset you and make you suspect the position was not what you had imagined it to be?"

"It . . . it was . . . this."

Now Udela reached for a bag which was attached by ribbons to her arm.

It was the kind of reticule that had been in

fashion some years previously and the Duke guessed that it was home-made.

Udela searched in silence, finding first a handkerchief, with which she surreptitiously wiped her eyes, before she took out a piece of paper.

She rose and handed it to the Duke, then sat down again on her chair.

The Duke saw at once that it was a cheaply printed leaflet which he suspected had been despatched to a great number of his friends and those who belonged to the Clubs in St. James's.

There had doubtless been one addressed to him, but his Comptroller would not have troubled to show it to him.

His lips curled scornfully as he read:

Mrs. Crawley presents her most respectful compliments to her Patrons and has pleasure in informing them that she has just received, at 27 Hay Hill, a consignment of unsurpassed Beauties from France, trained in every device and exotic allurement desired by those who are expert in the Sciences Galantes.

She also has for the delectation of her special Clients several dewy-eyed young Daisies straight from the Country, as young and fresh as the flowers they represent.

"Where did you find this?" the Duke asked.

"It was ... tucked down in the ... seat in the carriage," Udela answered. "I do not know what made me ... read it, except that ... once the carriage had started off, I thought it seemed ... foolish that I had no idea of the ... address where I would be staying."

"Surely Lord Julius's letter to you carried an address?"

"He wrote from his Club," Udela replied. "I think it was called 'White's.' "

The Duke's lips tightened.

He was growing more angry every moment at learning why his brother had seemed lately to have an unusual amount of money.

He knew now what Lady Marlene had been implying when with misplaced loyalty he had refused to listen to what she had been trying to tell him.

Ever since he had inherited the title and his father's fortune, his brother Julius had been a constant thorn in his flesh, resenting his position as head of the family but at the same time determined to exploit it to his own advantage.

He had paid up Julius's debts for him a dozen times, but despite every promise of being more careful in the future, he always came back for more.

He had also been involved in a great many unsavory incidents from which the Duke had been obliged to extricate him, merely in order to save the family name.

But he had never imagined that any man bearing the name of Westry would sink so low as to become a procurer for a bawdy-house.

What annoyed him more than anything else was the knowledge that what was happening had been deliberately kept from him by his friends.

He supposed that they were too embarrassed to tell him what Julius was doing, but he remembered now the warning glances that had been exchanged between them when Mrs. Crawley's name was mentioned.

He was aware too that the conversation had often faded into uncomfortable silence when he joined a group of men, or the subject would quickly be changed from the one on which they had been speaking.

A new House of Pleasure was always discussed and criticized by members of the Clubs, and he realised now that in his presence very little had been said about Mrs. Crawley's, which had opened only three or four months ago.

He was well aware that the women who catered to the more aristocratic of the Bucks and Beaux charged exorbitant sums, and although it had never amused him to visit such places, he had on occasion been pressured into joining a party of his friends, especially at the houses where, besides women, there was gaming.

He knew that to open what were often termed Palaces of Pleasure cost a great deal of capital, and he imagined with a feeling of rising fury that to raise such a sum Julius would have borrowed from Usurers, as he had done before, on his chances of inheriting the Dukedom.

The anger he was feeling must have shown in his face, for from the other side of the hearth-rug a frightened little voice said:

"You . . . are . . . angry . . . I am . . . sorry if any-thing I have said has . . . upset you."

"I am only angry," he replied, controlling his voice, "that a young and innocent girl should be tricked into coming to London."

"I thought it . . . must be one of the . . . wicked places which Papa sometimes warned the village-girls to avoid."

"Why should he do that?" the Duke enquired.

"Some of them wished to work in London in a nobleman's house, because the money was better than they could obtain in the country."

"I see—so your father made enquiries on their behalf?"

"Yes, indeed. He was very careful to do that, and he had also heard stories that when they arrived, they were sometimes met by evil women who offered them a lift in a comfortable carriage. Then they were never seen again."

"So you thought this was happening to you?" the Duke asked.

"I never imagined ... I never dreamt that a friend of ... Lord Eldridge would do anything of the sort ... but when I read what was written on the leaflet ... I was ... frightened."

"And quite rightly so."

Udela drew in her breath.

"Then when the ... carriage stopped ... " she said, and her voice faded away.

"That, I imagine, was when you reached the house in Hay Hill," the Duke said. "What upset you?"

"There were many ... lights and the door was open ... and I saw ... g-gentlemen with top-hats and satin-lined cloaks going in, and there was the ... sound of music."

"So you were suspicious that it was the place that was described in this leaflet!"

"I was ... wondering ... what to do," Udela said. "Then a servant came to the carriage and said to the footman who had got down from the box: 'Take her round to the back, you fool!' "

Udela made a sound that was almost a cry.

"I was sure then ... absolutely sure ... that the place was not a ... private house but ... wrong and ... wicked."

"What did you do?"

"I opened the ... door on the ... other side of the carriage and ... jumped out. As I started to ... run down the street ... I heard one of the servants shout! I knew they were ... chasing after me and ... I ran and ran ... until I saw ... you!"

Her voice broke with a fear that was still very real. Then she said:

"Thank you . . . thank you for . . . saving me . . . I know God must have . . . helped to . . . rescue me at the last moment."

The handkerchief went up to her eyes again.

She was being very brave, the Duke thought, after an ordeal that would be terrifying for any girl, especially one who, living in the country, had never come in contact with anything so unpleasant before.

He knew that she had been right when she said the women procurers of the bawdy-houses, both expensive and cheap ones, made a practice of meeting young girls at the Posting-Inns.

They would entice them in a carriage with the promise of a better place of work and then keep them drugged or terrorised until they no longer wished to escape.

Udela had in fact been very lucky, and looking at her now the Duke could understand why his disgraceful brother had thought she would be an asset at Mrs. Crawley's.

She certainly had a loveliness which was unusual, and there was something very fresh, innocent, and untouched about her which made her look younger than her eighteen years.

She had a grace that one might have expected to find amongst the ballet-dancers of Covent Garden, and there was also something very refined and aristocratic about the perfection of her features and the delicacy of her hands.

Looking at the sensitivity of her large eyes, the Duke thought he could not imagine anyone more unsuited to the sort of life his brother had intended her to lead.

At the same time, her beauty would understandably have tempted him to exploit her, and he wondered how she would fare without someone to look after her in a world where she must earn her own living.

As if she knew what he was thinking, Udela said in a frightened little voice:

"I would not ... wish to ... impose upon you any ... further, Sir, but I must ... find somewhere to ... stay the night ... and all my ... luggage was left in the carriage."

"I can find you somewhere for tonight," the Duke replied. "But what are you planning to do tomorrow?"

She made a helpless little gesture with her hands before she said:

"I suppose I must go ... home to Little Storton. It will be impossible for me to ... stay at the ... Vicarage. But I am sure there will be ... someone in the village who will let me ... lodge with them, until I can find ... somewhere else to go."

"You have some money?" the Duke asked.

She looked down at her hands and he saw the colour flood into her face.

"You must tell me the truth, Miss Hayward," he said. "I can only help you if you are truthful."

"I would not wish to be an ... encumbrance on a ... stranger," she said hesitatingly.

"I think it would be better," the Duke said with a faint smile, "if you thought of me as your rescuer rather than a stranger, and if I am to help you further, I must know your exact circumstances."

"My father owed quite a lot of money when he ... died," Udela said. "I sold the furniture, and I think, because the villagers loved him, they gave me more than the things were actually worth, but in the ... end there was very ... little left."

"How much?" the Duke asked bluntly.

"Only . . . nine pounds."

"And you had to pay your fare to London?"

"Yes. But I still have six pounds."

"And that is everything you have in the world?"

"I . . . am afraid so. Papa was ill for several months before he . . . died and the medicine and food the Doctor prescribed for him was . . . rather . . . expensive."

She looked at the Duke as she spoke, and he had the feeling that she was trying to tell him she had not been extravagant but had spent only what was absolutely necessary.

"So, all that stands between you and starvation," he said after a moment, "is six pounds."

"I am . . . sure I can find . . . some work."

She did not sound very confident and the Duke could hear still lurking beneath the surface the terror she felt when she had run away.

He rose without speaking to refill his glass from the bottle of champagne which stood in the crested ice-bucket on the grog-tray.

He glanced at Udela's glass and saw that it was still half-full. Then he said, as if he had just thought of it:

"Are you hungry? Would you care for something to eat?"

"No . . . thank you . . . I had some bread and cheese at the last place where the coach changed horses. There was a full meal for the passengers who could . . . afford it, but bread and cheese was all I . . . required."

"It would be no trouble to get you something now."

"I must not . . . impose on your hospitality any . . . further."

The Duke saw her give a quick glance round

the room as she spoke, then her eyes came back to him.

He knew that for the first time she was thinking that she was alone with a man she had never met before.

Carrying his glass of champagne in his hand, the Duke walked to stand in his habitual position, with his back to the fireplace.

Because it was summer, instead of a log-fire, the fireplace was massed with plants and flowers that had been brought up from Oswestry House in Kent.

The Duke did not notice the fragrance of them nor for the moment was he even aware that they existed.

He was only vividly conscious that Udela, still sitting very upright on the edge of her chair, was looking at him with wide, questioning eyes, and her whole body was tense.

"I have something to suggest to you," he said after a moment, "but first let me tell you that you can stay here tonight and my Housekeeper will look after you."

"S-stay ... here?" Udela repeated almost beneath her breath.

"You will not only be waited on by my staff," the Duke said, "but, as it happens, you will be competently chaperoned. My grandmother, the Dowager Duchess of Oswestry, arrived this afternoon, like you, from the country."

Udela gave a little gasp. Then she said in a hesitating voice:

"Do you ... do you mean that you are a ... Duke?"

"Yes. I am the Duke of Oswestry."

"I think I have ... heard of you ... but of course ... I might have guessed ..."

"Guessed?" the Duke enquired.

"You look so ... important, so magnificent ... that you could only be a ... Duke or a ... Royal Prince."

The Duke laughed.

He knew that Udela, speaking ingenuously, was not flattering him but just saying, as a child might do, what came into her mind.

It struck him that it was perhaps the most sincere compliment he had ever received.

"Thank you," he said, "but I think I had better tell you that Lord Julius Westry is in fact my brother!"

Now the sound Udela made was very different from the one she had made before. It was a cry of horror and also of fear, and, as if she was ready to run away once again, she rose to her feet.

"I want to apologise," the Duke went on quietly, "for my brother's appalling behaviour and to ask you to believe me when I say that I will do everything not only to help you but to make reparation for what you have suffered."

He knew as she stood looking at him that she was trying to decide whether she should believe him or whether she should try to escape as she had done before.

Then his eyes met hers and he knew, with a perception which he had not expected, that she felt that she could trust him and there was no reason for her to be so afraid.

He could almost read the thoughts flashing through her mind, which were mirrored in her strange grey eyes that seemed for the moment to fill the whole of her small face.

"You ... really ... mean that?" she asked in a voice he could barely hear.

"I promise you I am both ashamed of and humiliated by my brother's behaviour, and this is not the first time."

As if there was no need for her to reply, Udela sat down again.

Then she asked anxiously:

"You are sure it . . . would not be a terrible . . . nuisance for me to . . . stay here? I have . . . no wish to be any . . . trouble."

"You will be no trouble," the Duke replied.

He pulled at the bell as he spoke, and when the door opened only a second or so later, he said:

"Tell Mrs. Field that Miss Hayward will be staying here tonight and that her luggage has unfortunately been lost during her journey to London."

"Very good, Your Grace."

"And tell Mrs. Field I will send for her shortly to escort Miss Hayward to her room."

As the footman shut the door, Udela said:

"Thank you. Thank you . . . very much."

"Now will you listen to the suggestion I have for you?" the Duke asked.

"Of . . . course."

"It is difficult to put into words," he said, "but I am trying not only to help you but also to help myself, and it may seem a little strange."

"It would be . . . wonderful if I could . . . help you, after you have been so . . . kind to me."

"I think that, owing to my brother's behaviour, I am more in your debt than you in mine," the Duke replied. "But let us forget that for the moment and remember that when you leave here you have nowhere to go and, if we are honest, not much prospect of finding a reasonable or comfortable position where you can earn money."

"I have counted my . . . talents over and over

... again," Udela said, "and I am ... afraid they are not very ... saleable."

"I think most people would feel the same if unexpectedly they had to earn their own living."

"It is, however, rather ... shaming when Papa was so ... insistent that I should be well educated ... and Mama taught me to ... play the piano, although not well enough to be a professional pianist."

"I do not think the concert-platform or the stage is the right sort of life for you," the Duke said drily.

"I can cook," Udela told him. "I used to cook special dishes that Papa liked which were beyond the powers of old Mrs. Gibbs, who worked for us, but I do not suppose anyone would want me as a Chef."

"I cannot visualise you in a kitchen."

"As it ... appears I cannot be a ... Governess or work as a servant ... what can I ... do?"

As Udela finished speaking, the Duke knew that she was thinking of Lord Julius's solution to her problem.

He saw the fear come back into her eyes and she clenched her fingers together very tightly as if to prevent herself crying out once again at the horror of it.

"What I am going to suggest," he said quietly, "is something very different."

Udela was listening, and he paused as if he was choosing his words very carefully before he said:

"I am in an uncomfortable position which I do not wish to explain, but it would help me considerably if I could make it clear to the world, and to one person in particular, why it would be impossible for me to marry her."

Udela looked puzzled, but she did not speak and the Duke went on:

"It suddenly struck me, when you were talking, that if you would consent for a short period to pretend we were betrothed, it would in fact solve both your problem and mine."

He saw her eyes widen and he said quickly:

"Let me make it clear that there will be no question of marriage. I have no intention of marrying anybody within a great number of years at any rate, but if I could produce someone to whom I am engaged and make my friends believe that it is a genuine attachment, it would, as I have already said, set me free from a difficult and uncomfortable situation."

"You . . . mean it would . . . really help you?"

"Very much."

"Then of course . . . I would do anything you asked me to do. But would your friends believe . . . that you could in any circumstances have become betrothed to . . . someone like me?"

Udela spoke humbly and the Duke smiled.

"You cannot have looked in the mirror, Miss Hayward—or should I say Udela?—if you question any man's reason for wishing to marry you."

"B-but I am very . . . unimportant and not . . . smart like the ladies who I am sure are your . . . usual companions."

As she spoke, she was thinking of the sketches she had seen in the Ladies' Magazine which her mother would sometimes buy, and of the guests who had stayed at Eldridge House when the present Squire's mother was living there.

She had always thought when she saw them in Church, wearing sables in the winter and pelisses of satin or taffeta in the summer, that they looked like visitors from another world.

As she thought of them, she was acutely aware of the contrast between the plain, serviceable gown which she had made herself and the luxury and beauty of the room in which she and the Duke were sitting.

As if once again the Duke followed her thoughts, he said:

"I promise you that if you will consent to be presented to the world as my future wife, you will have the right clothes to wear for the part you will play."

"You mean . . . that *you* will . . . give them to . . . me?" Udela said hesitatingly.

"I can hardly expect you to provide them out of the six pounds which you tell me is your whole fortune."

Udela did not answer. She turned her head to look across the room, and her profile with its straight little nose and firm chin was silhouetted against the bookcase behind her.

'She is lovely,' the Duke thought to himself. 'So lovely that no one will question for a moment that I should wish to marry her.'

Then, as if he sensed that something was wrong, he asked:

"What is troubling you?"

"I was just . . . thinking," Udela said, "that it would not be right for you to pay for my clothes. Perhaps you could . . . lend me a little money. I would not be . . . extravagant . . . then when I find some work to do . . . I could . . . pay you back."

For a moment the Duke thought she must be joking.

He had never yet met a woman, in whatever rank of society she moved, who was not prepared, because he was so rich, to extract the most expensive presents from him.

These, where his mistresses were concerned, invariably consisted of furs and jewels and gowns of every description.

"I see that I have not made myself plain," he said. "If you will act this part for me, you will of course be paid for your services exactly as if you were doing any other type of work. I am not quite certain for how long I shall require you to keep up the pretence, but let me say now that in consideration for your services, I am prepared not only to provide you with everything you require but, when we part, to give you the sum of one thousand pounds."

"One . . . thousand . . . pounds?"

Udela could hardly breathe the words, then she said quickly:

"No, of course not! I could not accept such a sum or anything like it!"

"On that point I do not intend to argue," the Duke said, "but let me prophesy that when you have been ostensibly my fiancée for a few months, or even weeks, it will seem so small a sum that you will demand more."

"How could you imagine for one moment that I could be so . . . ungrateful?" Udela asked. "But please . . . please . . . Your Grace . . . if you really intend to give me so much, then I can quite easily pay for my own gowns."

"Again you must allow me to have my own way," the Duke replied. "In fact, that must be included in our contract."

As he spoke, he had the idea that since he had been so often tricked, deceived, and blackmailed in the past, he would make sure that on this occasion it would not happen again.

"What I am going to do," he said, "is to write down exactly what I require of you, and you will

sign it. Then we can be sure that when finally you
leave me to lead your own life, there will be no
repercussions and, I hope, no recriminations."

"How could you . . . imagine for a . . . moment
that there . . . would be?" Udela enquired. "But
please, Your Grace, are you quite certain you want
me to do this?"

"Quite certain."

"It would really help you . . . you are not just
being . . . kind to me?"

"I assure you that I am a very selfish person
and am thinking of myself first and foremost."

As he turned back from his desk, he thought
her eyes searched his face as if to assure herself
that he was sincere.

"Suppose I . . . fail you and . . . make a mess of
everything?"

"I do not think you will do that."

"You realise I am . . . very inexperienced and I
have . . . never met anybody like you?"

The Duke was certain that this was true, but before he could answer, Udela went on:

"Before the late Lord and Lady Eldridge died,
I used to go with Papa and Mama to their garden-
parties and sometimes for luncheon or tea, but they
were the only grand people I knew, and Papa did
not approve of the new Lord Eldridge or his . . .
friends."

As she spoke, Udela realised that one of those
friends was the Duke's brother, and the colour rose
in her face again and she looked uncomfortable.

Quickly, as if she wished to hide her embarrass-
ment, she said:

"I shall . . . make mistakes . . . and you will be
. . . ashamed of me."

"I am quite certain that you will not make many
mistakes," the Duke said. "I will be with you to

look after you, and I promise you it will not be such an ordeal as it sounds. In fact, after the engagement is announced and we have made a few appearances, we might go to the country."

Udela's eyes lit up.

"That would be . . . wonderful!"

The Duke, however, was thinking that it would be a mistake for Lady Marlene, once she had recovered from the shock of the engagement, to have time to attack him again.

He had the feeling that she would not give in too easily. All the same, he was well aware that if he was engaged to be married, it would be very difficult for Lady Marlene's brother, the Earl of Stanwick, to make the scene which he could otherwise do.

It was one thing for the Earl to insist that the Duke should marry his sister, but quite another to expect an official betrothal to be broken in order to do so.

Anything spiteful, unkind, or defamatory that the Earl or Lady Marlene might say about him would, the Duke thought, be attributed to jealousy.

Also, if for three months they never appeared anywhere together in public and all his friends knew of her liaison with Lord Nazeby, it was doubtful that anyone would believe her if she insisted that the baby she was carrying was the responsibility of her previous lover.

The Duke was not sure how the idea had come to him that this was the way out he had been seeking, but he thought that perhaps it was not only because Udela was so helpless and so alone in the world but because she was so lovely.

His long experience with women had taught him that, dressed in the fashionable manner, she would be able to hold her own with all the famous and much-toasted "Incomparables."

They had been acclaimed and eulogised until most men, like himself, were heartily sick of hearing their names.

He somehow knew that anybody as young and unspoilt as Udela would be a novelty. Moreover, they would find it almost incredible that she had captured the most elusive and the most sought-after bachelor in the whole country.

He thought triumphantly that it was a brilliant answer to Lady Marlene's demand that he should marry her, besides being a very effective answer to Udela's dilemma.

'I am even cleverer than I thought I was,' he thought as he sat down at his desk.

His good fortune had not failed him, and he had solved the insoluble.

He drew from a drawer a piece of thick parchment writing-paper embellished with his crest, and opened the red leather blotter, also embellished in gold with his coat-of-arms.

He dipped a newly cut quill pen into the exquisitely chased gold ink-pot which had been fashioned by a great craftsman in the reign of Charles II and began to write.

Behind him, Udela looked at his head silhouetted against the light from the candelabrum, and thought she must be in a dream.

It could not be true that she had come to London to find that a gentleman like Lord Julius Westry had been prepared to commit her to a life of sin, or that she should be rescued by a Duke.

Now she was agreeing to a proposal which she could hardly believe had not come only from her imagination.

How could it be possible for one moment that

she could pretend to be the fiancée of the man who sat in front of her writing, or that anyone would believe such a pretence?

She had never known that any man could look so handsome or so overwhelmingly important.

When she had first come with him into the Library, she had been too terror-stricken to be aware of anything except that he had saved her from the men who were pursuing her and would have taken her back to that gaudily lit house which she had known was as evil as hell itself.

Now that her heart had stopped thumping and she was not trembling, she could look at him and knew that he was in fact what her father would have called "a great gentleman."

'I think Papa would have approved of him,' she thought to herself, and yet still she was not sure.

Could anything be more fantastic than what he had suggested?

The mere fact that he was prepared not only to pay for her clothes but to give her such an enormous sum of money raised an intimidating question:

What else would he ask of her?

Despite the fact that she had worked in the village with her father amongst the poor inhabitants, Udela was very innocent.

She knew, of course, that young girls got into trouble with men, that babies were born without fathers, that respectable people had a nasty name for them, and that their mothers were treated like pariahs.

But she was not certain what the word "sin" in that particular context involved. She did not know what the men, especially those who looked like Lord Julius, did, or what took place in bawdy-houses.

She knew that gentlemen paid for their pleasures, which she thought was wicked in itself, for how could a man buy love, which should be given freely and from the heart?

It was all very puzzling, and as she sat trying to think it all out, trying to understand what was happening, she suddenly felt very tired. She knew it was because she had stayed up very late last night packing what was left in the Vicarage.

Then, after only two hours in her bed, she had been forced to rise and dress to catch the stage-coach when it passed the crossroads at the end of the village.

She had a sudden longing to lie down, and even as she knew it was ridiculous to think of such a thing, when there were so many important decisions to be made, the Duke turned round in his chair.

"Come here, Udela!"

She rose and went to his side.

"I want you to read what I have written," he said, "then sign it."

He handed her a piece of writing-paper as he spoke, and she saw that it was inscribed with strong, upright handwriting which she felt was exactly the way the Duke would write.

"Read it aloud!" he ordered.

In a soft, musical voice, Udela obeyed him.

"I, Udela Hayward, agree that I will assume the role of fiancée to His Grace the Duke of Oswestry for as long as he wishes me to remain in that capacity. I will tell no one that this is only a 'pretence' engagement to suit both His Grace's convenience and my own, but will behave with every propriety and in an exemplary manner until His Grace releases me from the commitment to him which I have undertaken. For my services

in this respect I have agreed to accept the sum of one thousand pounds and not to ask for any other recompense, but when the time comes to leave immediately and without complaint. To this Agreement, made willingly and at my own wish, on this 10th day of June, 1820, I hereby sign my name."

Udela's voice faltered into silence. Then she said:

"You are sure ... quite sure, Your Grace, that you wish to give me such an ... enormous sum of money?"

"It will enable you to live quietly and in comfort for several years," the Duke replied.

"Longer than that," Udela said. "You do realise that Papa's stipend was only three hundred pounds a year, and he always considered it a very generous one."

"Then I am sure the one thousand pounds I shall give you," the Duke smiled, "will last you until you are married to someone of your own choice."

"It still ... seems too ... much," Udela said almost beneath her breath.

"I have told you I have no wish to argue about it," the Duke said sharply, "and if you have no more comments to make, I suggest you sign this document, and I shall keep it in a safe place which no one except you and I will know about."

As he spoke, he thought that this should preclude any difficulties when their pretence engagement came to an end.

No one would be surprised, he told himself, if he broke off an engagement as easily as he had broken off his many liaisons, as he had done continuously and frequently over the last few years.

In the meantime, he would undoubtedly cause a

sensation by producing Udela, as it were, out of the blue, and anything that Lady Marlene might say would certainly sink into insignificance.

'I have been very clever!' the Duke thought to himself with satisfaction as he handed Udela the quill-pen.

He also vacated his chair so that she could sit down, and now she hesitated, almost as if she was afraid to sign the paper that lay in front of her, before she inscribed her name.

As she did so, the Duke saw that her handwriting was as delicate and graceful as she was herself.

He took the paper from her and put it in a drawer, which he then locked. Then he crossed the room and rang the bell.

"I hope you will sleep well, Udela," he said. "Tomorrow you shall meet my grandmother and she will arrange for the dressmakers to come and measure you. You understand I would not wish you to appear in public until you are dressed for the part."

He smiled, then added as if he thought it would make her feel more reassured:

"You will be my leading-lady in a drama which concerns us both, and I am quite certain that once the first shock is over, you will enjoy the role."

"I will do my best . . . my very . . . very best to please you," Udela said in a nervous little voice.

He saw the sincerity in her eyes as he looked down at her, and he thought it would be very difficult for her to lie or indeed to be anything but straight-forward and honest.

He could not remember ever before having seen a woman's eyes that were so expressive and mirrored every passing thought.

"You . . . will . . . help me?" Udela asked.

"In every way I can."

The door opened and the Housekeeper stood

there, who, the Duke was well aware, must have been aroused from her bed to attend him.

She was a woman nearing sixty, with grey hair and an authority which made the younger maids quake in their shoes.

At the same time, the Duke knew that Mrs. Field was largely instrumental in keeping his London house running with the smooth efficiency he demanded of all his possessions.

She curtsyed and said:

"Good-evening, Your Grace."

"Good-evening, Mrs. Field. I regret having to disturb you at so late an hour, but I wish you to look after Miss Hayward, who arrived in London after a series of mishaps which finally resulted in her losing all her luggage."

"I'm sorry to hear that, Miss."

Mrs. Field dropped a curtsey to Udela, but it was not so low or so respectful as the one she had accorded to her employer.

"Good-night, Udela," the Duke said. "I feel sure that after all your adventures, you will sleep well, and do not worry about anything."

"I will . . . try not to, Your Grace."

Udela curtsyed, then as she rose she said in a voice that only the Duke could hear:

"Thank you from the . . . bottom of my . . . heart. I know . . . God sent you to . . . help me."

Chapter Three

Udela awoke feeling that she had slept for a very long time, and she realised that what had aroused her was someone pulling back the curtains.

For a moment she could not think where she was, then she remembered what had happened last night and felt a little tremor run through her.

She was not sure whether it was excitement or fear!

It had been impossible when she went to bed not to remember the terror she had experienced when she had realised to what sort of place she had been brought in Lord Julius's carriage.

Then she forced herself to think of the kindness of the Duke and the fact that she was now safe in his impressive house and being chaperoned by his grandmother.

But even that was frightening!

What would the Dowager think when her grandson, who was so important and distinguished, told her he intended to marry a Vicar's daughter from the country?

However, it was reassuring to recall that the Duke had said that she was helping him and that he was selfish enough for that to be his chief concern.

"If I can help him," Udela told herself, "I shall feel . . . justified in allowing him to . . . pay for my clothes."

At the same time, she was sure it was wrong for any gentleman to provide a lady with anything so intimate as what she wore.

Then sensibly she asked herself what the alternative was. She could hardly appear as the Duke's fiancée in the only gown she possessed.

Even if she had not lost those that were in her trunk, they certainly would not have been suitable to wear in the company of someone as grand as the Duke.

She now realised that the maid, who had finished drawing the curtains, had placed a table beside her bed and set on it a tray containing her breakfast.

There was a silver coffee-pot embellished with the Duke's crest, a covered silver dish, and porcelain cups and plates so exquisite that Udela felt they should be in a cabinet and not in daily use.

Because she was aware that she felt hungry, she sat up against her pillows to thank the maid, in a soft, shy voice, for bringing her breakfast.

"If there's anything else you wants, Miss," the maid said, "you've only to ring the bell. I'll be listening for it."

"Thank you," Udela replied.

As she looked again at the tray she thought it would be impossible for anybody to want more.

There was toast in a silver rack, there was a large peach with a gold knife and fork with which to eat it, and there were small dishes of exquisite workmanship to hold pats of Jersey butter and home-made marmalade.

'I do wish Mama could see this,' Udela thought.

Looking round the room, she realised it was more beautiful than any room she had ever imagined.

She was just finishing the last mouthful of the peach when there was a knock on the door and Mrs. Field came in.

"I hope you slept well, Miss."

"Very well, thank you," Udela replied. "I think I must have been very tired."

"I'm sure you were, Miss, after such a nasty experience of being so delayed on the roads and then losing your luggage."

Udela did not answer and the Housekeeper went on:

"I've pressed the gown you were wearing, Miss. I'm afraid you'll find it too warm for such a sunny day, but there's nothing else I can offer you."

"I shall be all right," Udela replied, "and thank you for the nightgown you loaned me last night. It is a very beautiful one."

Of fine lawn inset with lace, she was sure, although Mrs. Field had not said so, that it must belong to the Duke's grandmother.

"Annie's preparing your bath, Miss," Mrs. Field said, "and when you're dressed, His Grace would like to speak to you in the Library."

"His . . . Grace!" Udela exclaimed almost beneath her breath.

"There's no need to hurry, Miss," Mrs. Field said. "His Grace has gone riding and he's not expected back for at least half-an-hour."

"I will get up at once!" Udela said nervously.

As she bathed and dressed she wondered fran-

tically if the Duke wished to see her to tell her that
after all he had changed his mind.

She had heard that gentlemen often said things
at night, after a good dinner and perhaps too much
wine, which they afterwards regretted.

The Duke had certainly seemed entirely sober,
but, she told herself, she was so inexperienced
where men were concerned that he might have
made the suggestion of their pretended engagement
only to wake in the cold light of morning to regret
it.

"If that is what he intends," Udela told herself
nervously, "what shall I ... do? How shall I ...
manage?"

Last night, because the Duke had been kind, she
had gone to bed feeling that in Oswestry House, if
nowhere else, she was safe and protected.

But now she was afraid that she might find herself back in the streets, without that protection. In
which case, to whom could she turn for help?

The sensible thing would be to return at once to
Little Storton.

Perhaps when the new Vicar arrived she could
ask him to help her, and she was sure that one of
the cottagers would give her a bed if there was nowhere else she could go.

It would be humiliation to have to rely on their
generosity, and she was afraid of the attitude that
Lord Eldridge might take if his friend Lord Julius
complained that she had run away.

"What can I do? What can I do?" she asked herself.

As she walked across the Hall to the Library
where she had been with the Duke the night before, she found herself praying that he would still
want her to stay.

A footman opened the door, saying:

"His Grace only returned a few minutes ago, Miss, and is having breakfast. I'll say you're waiting for him."

"Thank you," Udela replied faintly.

She walked across the room and saw that now the curtains were drawn and the garden outside the windows was ablaze with colour.

It made her feel homesick for Little Storton and her mother.

'If only I could put the clock back,' she wished, as many people had before her.

She must have stood looking out at the flowers for quite a long time before she heard the door open and turned with a nervous little start to see the Duke come into the room.

He was wearing riding-clothes, white buckskin breeches, polished boots, and a smart cut-away riding-coat, and she thought he seemed a little less formidable than he had the night before.

But she was really looking at his face, wondering what he had to say to her, worrying in a way that made her heart beat frantically in case he should say that after all he had no need of her services.

He walked towards her and she saw that he was smiling.

"You slept well, I hope?"

Udela curtsyed.

"Yes . . . thank you . . . Your Grace."

"I wanted to see you as soon as you were awake and before I saw anybody else, because there are certain important details we forgot last night."

"F-forgot?"

Udela's voice was a little unsteady and she thought with a sudden lift of her heart that apparently he had not changed his mind.

"The first thing people are likely to ask us," the Duke said, "is where we met each other. That is easy to answer, because I frequently stay in Huntingdonshire, not with Lord Eldridge but with the Earl of Huntingdon."

Udela did not speak. She was looking at the Duke, her eyes very wide, and, because while waiting she had been so anxious as to what he would say, she looked pale.

"I thought it would seem reasonable," the Duke went on, "to say we met nearly a year ago when you were only seventeen, and that while we had a fondness for each other, I thought you were too young to be married."

The Duke paused for a moment, as if he was planning it out in his mind, then he continued:

"When I heard that your father was dead and you were alone in the world, I knew it was the right moment to announce our engagement. Does that sound plausible?"

"Y-yes . . . yes . . . of course, Your Grace."

Udela was so relieved to learn that she need no longer be afraid of being sent away that her voice sounded strange even to herself.

The Duke looked at her for a moment, then asked:

"What has been worrying you? I thought when I came into the room that you looked perturbed."

He looked into her eyes, and her lashes were very dark against her cheeks.

"I . . . I was afraid that you had . . . changed your mind and were . . . sending me away."

"I never change my mind," the Duke said positively. "When I say I shall do something, you can rely on me to do it."

"I am . . . sorry," Udela said quickly. "It was . . . just that last night it was so . . . wonderful of you to . . . save me and to know that you were . . . prepared to . . . protect me from . . ."

"Forget it," the Duke interrupted. "We must forget everything that happened last night, and I have already told my Butler that if any servants talk about what occurred they will be instantly dismissed."

He spoke so sternly that Udela drew in her breath.

She was still aware that even though she could trust the Duke, there was something very formidable about him.

"I have told you what I intend to say," the Duke said, "but there are one or two other details which are important."

As he spoke, he walked towards his desk and sat down in the same chair in which he had written out their contract last night.

"First," he said, "I must know your father's full name and a little about his family."

"Papa was Henry Lionel Hayward," Udela answered. "His family came from Northumberland. His father was always known as 'Squire Hayward.'"

"I imagine he was not very well off."

"He owned quite a lot of land, but it was not very productive. And Papa had two brothers, so there was nothing for him to inherit."

"You did not think of going to stay with your relatives now that your father is dead?"

"My father was the youngest," Udela replied, "and both his brothers are dead. As they lived so far away from us I have never met their wives and families."

The Duke looked down at the piece of paper on which he had written her father's name.

"And who was your mother before she married?"

"Elizabeth Massingburgh. Her father was Major-General Sir Alexander Massingburgh."

The Duke wrote down the names of Udela's mother and grandfather, then raised his head.

"You mean the General who was so successful in India?"

"He was my grandfather, but I met him only once."

"Why was that?"

"He was very angry with Mama for not marrying 'into the Regiment' as he had wished. There was a suitor whom my grandfather favoured, but Mama had fallen in love with my father."

"So I suppose he was not very generous," the Duke reasoned.

"No, indeed. He gave Mama a small allowance over the years, and when I was nine he asked her to come and see him when he was home on leave from India . . ."

As she spoke, Udela could remember how authoritative and overpowering her grandfather had seemed when her mother had taken her to meet him at a Hotel in London.

She remembered being surprised that her mother did not kiss the Major-General but merely curtsyed to him as he said abruptly:

"I sent for you, Elizabeth, to ask you to come back with me to India. I have been appointed Governor of Madras and I want a hostess."

Udela remembered that her mother had smiled as if she thought her father was being rather stupid. Then she had said quietly:

"I am very honoured, Papa, that you should want me in that capacity, but I could not leave my husband or Udela."

"Udela—and I consider that a ridiculous name for a child—can come with you."

"And my husband?"

"If you imagine I would allow him to set foot in

any house of mine, you are very much mistaken!"

Udela remembered there was a little pause before her mother had said:

"I would have liked to be with you, Papa, and to see India. It would have given me great pleasure, but as I am sure you have already anticipated, my answer must be no."

"You would live in great luxury," the Major-General had said sharply. "My position as Governor is a very important one, not unlike that of Royalty in any other country. It would be an experience you would never forget."

Udela's mother had given a little sigh.

"It sounds fascinating, Papa, but there are two things that you cannot offer me."

Udela remembered that her grandfather had not asked what they were. He had merely waited for her mother to tell him.

"Happiness and love!" Mrs. Hayward had said softly.

They had stayed for nearly an hour but Udela had known her grandfather was angry.

She had not been surprised, when he died five years later, to learn that he had left her mother only the small allowance he had given her during his lifetime, with the proviso that when she died it should cease immediately.

Udela explained the position briefly to the Duke. She had the feeling he was pleased that her grandfather had been of some importance in the world.

"The notice of our engagement will be in the *Gazette* tomorrow morning," he said. "And now I want to take you up to meet my grandmother."

"Will she not think it strange that you have become . . . engaged so suddenly?"

"She will certainly be surprised," the Duke answered, "but since most grandmothers wish their grandsons to be married so that they can 'settle down,' she will undoubtedly be delighted."

There was a sarcastic note in his voice which told Udela all too clearly that he had been pressed in the past to choose a wife.

She could understand, she told herself, that there must be a great many women wanting to marry him, and she wondered what the uncomfortable circumstances were which made him wish to have a "pretence" engagement rather than a real one.

She felt curious but was certain that it was something she would never learn, and when the Duke put down his pen and rose from his desk, she followed him across the room.

They went upstairs and walked along the corridor without speaking. Then the Duke knocked on a door and at the same time opened it.

They entered a sunlit *Boudoir* in which there were so many flowers it looked like a bower.

Lying on a *chaise-longue* by the window, an ermine rug covering her feet, was a woman who Udela knew must have been very beautiful when she was young.

Even though she had white hair and wrinkled skin, she was still lovely and had a distinction which Udela was sure was related not only to her appearance but to her personality.

"Good-morning, Randolph! This is a surprise!" the Dowager said as the Duke crossed the room and lifted her hand to his lips.

"I am calling earlier than usual, Grandmama," he replied, "because I wish you to be the first to know of Udela's arrival here."

"Udela?" the Duchess questioned.

She looked with surprise in her eyes at Udela, who had followed the Duke a little way across the room.

She curtsyed and the Duke said:

"This is Udela Hayward, Grandmama, to whom I am announcing my engagement tomorrow morning!"

His grandmother gave a little cry.

"Your engagement? My dear boy—why did you not tell me?"

"Because," the Duke replied, "Udela arrived here unexpectedly last night, after a series of mishaps. First, I did not receive her letter telling me she was coming to London, and secondly, owing to an accident on the road, she did not reach the house until long after you had gone to bed."

"You poor child!" the Duchess exclaimed. "How tired you must have been! But you are engaged to my grandson! I can hardly believe it!"

She looked at the Duke as she spoke, as if to confirm that it was the truth, and he said with a slightly mocking smile:

"You have bullied me long enough, Grandmama, so you should be glad that after a great deal of evasion I have obeyed your instructions."

"Glad? Of course I am glad!" the Dowager cried. "But why have I never heard of this lovely girl before?"

"Her grandfather was Major-General Sir Alexander Massingburgh, of whom I am sure you have heard."

"But of course!" the Dowager said. "The hero of the Mahrattas wars! The Duke of Wellington was speaking of him only a few months ago when he was reminiscing about his days in India."

"You have a marvellously retentive memory, Grandmama," the Duke said, "and you never forget a name."

"It would be difficult to forget anyone so distinguished," the Duchess said with a smile, and added to Udela: "Come here, my child, and tell me how you have captured my most elusive grandson, who for years had sworn that he would never marry anyone, even though we have begged him to do so, on our bended knees."

Shyly, the colour rising in her cheeks, Udela moved nearer to the *chaise-longue* as she had been told to do.

"You are a lovely young woman!" the Dowager said with a note of approval in her voice. "I can understand why you have succeeded where so many others have failed."

"Thank ... you," Udela said in a very small voice.

She was feeling that it was wrong to deceive anyone so old and so beautiful as the Duchess.

As if the Duke was aware of what she was feeling, he said quickly:

"Now, Grandmama, we need your help. There is a great deal to be done."

"In what way?" the Duchess enquired.

"As Udela has been in mourning for her father for some months, she knew when she came to London that she required a whole new wardrobe. But, what is more, owing to the accident on the road to the carriage in which she was travelling, she has nothing at the moment but what she stands up in."

The Duchess gave a little cry of concern.

"Now I understand," she said, "why my lady's-maid told me that Mrs. Field had borrowed one of my nightgowns last night. I thought it was a strange thing for her to do."

"I was very grateful, Ma'am," Udela said.

"What I am suggesting," the Duke interposed, "is that you send immediately for the dressmakers, the milliners, and the whole caboodle to fit Udela out before the notice of our engagement appears in the *Gazette*."

"And when is that to be?" the Duchess enquired.

"Tomorrow morning."

The Duchess gave a cry.

"And you expect me to buy her a trousseau in that time?"

"I suggest you start by at least providing her with a nightgown of her own."

The Duchess laughed.

"Randolph, you are incorrigible! You have always been the same! Because you yourself can move mountains to get what you want, you expect the rest of us to be able to do the same!"

"Ever since I have known you, Grandmama," the Duke replied, "you have invariably got your own way even where I was concerned. So I know that I can be absolutely confident that when an influx of well-wishers appears tomorrow, Udela will be looking her best."

"If that is what you expect," the Duchess said sharply, "go away at once and send your Comptroller, Mr. Humphries, to me. I shall also want your footmen and your grooms to be ready to run all over London."

"You may have the whole household at your disposal," the Duke said with a laugh, "and thank you, Grandmama."

He bent and kissed her hand as he spoke, then with a smile at Udela he went from the room.

With difficulty she restrained an impulse to run after him and beg him not to leave her alone.

She was frightened—in a different way now from what she had been before, but she was still frightened.

How could the Duke speak so glibly of well-

wishers? Of her being dressed in twenty-four hours
to receive people who would all be intensely curious about her and of whom she knew nothing?

Then she realised that the Duchess was looking
at her with a twinkle in her eyes.

"The one thing I find more enjoyable than drinking a glass of champagne," she said, "is spending
money. I presume, as soldiers never have any, that
my grandson is to provide you with your trousseau."

Udela looked worried.

"I am sure it is . . . wrong, Ma'am. My mother,
if she was . . . alive, would be very . . . shocked at
the idea. But it is . . . true . . . I have no . . . money."

"That certainly need not perturb you, with Randolph's Bank Account to draw on," the Duchess
said.

"I would not wish to spend . . . more than is
absolutely . . . necessary," Udela said hastily.

"Nonsense!" the Duchess exclaimed. "After all
the fuss there has been about Randolph refusing
even to look at a marriageable woman, you will
have to look fantastic or no one will believe that
he has finally been captured."

It was as if, Udela thought uncomfortably, the
Duchess suspected that her grandson's engagement
was not exactly what it appeared to be.

Then she told herself that what the Dowager had
said was undoubtedly true.

She must look different, she must in fact be outstanding in some way, or else people might suspect
there was something strange behind such a precipi-
tate engagement.

It was surprising how quickly the dressmakers,
the milliners, the tailors, and the shoe-makers answered the calls to come to Oswestry House.

Bond Street was not far away. Even so, Udela

was sure that their eagerness was due to the fact that the Duke was not only very rich but also of tremendous importance.

When the Duchess explained that they were buying a trousseau, their smiles of congratulations and their excitement inevitably made Udela feel more guilty because she was acting a lie.

But she only had to remember that if it were not for the Duke, she would at this moment be in a very different position and only a street away from disaster.

She tried to recall the things that her father had said when he had warned young girls of the village of the dangers and temptations that awaited them in London.

Because she naturally had not been present at her father's interviews with the villagers who had been engaged either for Lord Eldridge's London house or for the houses of his friends and acquaintances, she could only think of what he had told her later.

"I am quite convinced," she remembered his saying once to her mother, "that Betty Geary is half-witted, and she is too pretty, in my opinion, to be allowed to go to London."

"Lady Eldridge has arranged for her to work for her cousin the Countess of Datchet," his wife had replied.

"I only hope the Cook or Housekeeper whom Betty works under will keep a strict eye on her," Udela's father had said in a worried tone. "I was hearing only the other day of the large number of girls from the country who disappear when they reach London. You know full well the type of house in which they are kept prisoner."

"It is terrible!" Mrs. Hayward had agreed. "But there is nothing you can do about it, dearest. You have quite enough problems in Little Storton without adding to them."

"If the City had more Police it would be better," Udela's father had continued, as if he was following his own train of thought. "At the moment, no young woman, whatever her class, can walk alone in safety, and anyone as pretty as Betty Geary is asking for trouble."

Her father had every right to be worried, Udela thought. For herself it had not been a question of finding dangers in the streets of London but in the lane outside the Church-yard at home.

It seemed incredible that Lord Julius Westry, brother of the Duke of Oswestry, should involve himself in anything so horrifying as having her taken to a house of ill repute.

'Had I not run away,' Udela thought, 'I should at this moment be there and would never have been able to escape.'

She felt a little shiver of horror run through her at the thought, and the Duchess said with concern:

"You are not cold, child?"

"No, no, of course not," Udela said quickly. "It was just what people in the village call 'a goose walking over my grave.' "

The Duchess laughed.

"I know the feeling, but you should have no morbid thoughts at the moment—only happy ones."

She paused before she said:

"I cannot tell you how happy I am that my grandson is to be married. I was afraid he would never get over something which happened when he was very young and which I have always thought turned him into the cynic he sometimes seems."

"What happened?" Udela asked.

"I am sure he would not like me to speak of it if he has not told you himself," the Duchess said.

"Anyway, he pretends it is something he has forgotten. But a girl with whom he was in love treated him very badly, and he was young and impressionable enough for it to leave a scar which I have sometimes thought would never heal."

The Duchess smiled before she added:

"Thank goodness I was wrong! Now he is to be married to you, and the whole family will rejoice when they learn of it tomorrow morning."

In between choosing the gowns and supervising the fittings of those to be altered for her to wear immediately, Udela was aware that the Duchess was writing notes that were to be taken to members of the family who lived in London.

"Our close relatives will be furious if they are not told before they see it in the *Gazette,*" she said several times during the day.

The Duke had not appeared at luncheon-time and they ate a light meal in the Duchess's *Boudoir*.

When the last dressmaker withdrew and Udela felt her legs were so tired they could not carry her any longer, the Duchess said:

"Personally, I have found it an exciting but very tiring day. I suppose it is very unconventional, but I shall allow you and Randolph to dine alone while I have dinner up here on a tray. I am going to bed."

"Oh, please . . . join us, Ma'am!" Udela pleaded.

She had the feeling that it might be difficult to be alone with the Duke. She thought too that he would find it boring, and in any case she had no idea how to cope with him.

"You cannot pretend that you do not want him to yourself," the Duchess said. "Go and lie down for a short time, child. Then put on that pretty gown which wanted less alteration than the others.

I would like to see you in it before you go down-stairs."

"Yes, of course, Ma'am," Udela replied, "and thank you for being so kind. I never thought I would ever own so many beautiful clothes. I only hope that when His Grace sees me in them he will know that his money has been well spent."

"I will leave him to tell you what he thinks," the Duchess said with a smile.

Udela went to her own room and, because she knew it was the sensible thing to do, lay down on her bed.

She found herself worrying because, whatever the reasons for her pretence engagement, it was hard for her to act convincingly and also to pretend, as she knew the Duchess expected, that she and the Duke were very much in love with each other.

When she was dressed and ready to go down-stairs for dinner, she looked at herself in the mirror and felt that at least she did not appear as unim-portant and insignificant as she was in reality.

The expensive white gown made her look very young and almost as if she were clothed in the soft clouds of a summer sky.

The maid had brushed her hair until it shone with a thousand gleaming lights, and she had had no idea until now what a perfect figure she had.

This was not only because the gown was skilfully and cleverly cut, but also because she was wearing beneath it a small corset that came, she had been told, from Paris.

It certainly gave her a more slender waist than she had suspected she had and at the same time an almost classical grace.

Dutifully, because she had been told to, she went first to show herself to the Duchess, but to her con-sternation when she entered the bedroom where the

Dowager was ensconced in a huge canopied bed, propped against several lace-trimmed pillows, she found that the Duke was there.

At her appearance the Duchess gave a little exclamation of pleasure.

"Now, Randolph, tell me if I have waved my magic wand and made Udela look as you wished."

"I have always suspected your magic powers, Grandmama," the Duke replied, "and now that I have positive proof of them, I am completely spellbound!"

Because Udela felt shy at finding him unexpectedly with his grandmother, she had not been able to look at him as she came into the room.

Now, feeling that both he and the Dowager were waiting for her to speak, she said:

"You are so . . . kind . . . and I am very . . . very . . . grateful!"

"I wish we had more time before presenting Udela to the family," the Duchess said. "All the same, I think they will understand why you have at last succumbed to an arrow from Eros."

"I would not have thought of putting it as elegantly as you do, Grandmama," the Duke replied, "but that, of course, is what has happened."

There was almost a mocking note in his voice which Udela thought was somewhat indiscreet.

She felt that she should warn him that some of his friends might think he was playing a joke on them!

Then, for the first time, and she thought it extremely stupid that she had not thought of it before, she realised that the one person who would be aware that the whole thing was a make-believe would be Lord Julius.

Because she felt she must tell the Duke at once

of her fears, she said as they left his grandmother's room to go down the stairs together:

"Could I . . . speak to you?"

"Of course," the Duke replied, "but dinner should be ready in a few moments!"

"This will not take long."

She thought perhaps she should wait until the meal was over. At the same time, she knew that because she was worried it would be impossible to eat anything until she had told the Duke what she feared.

They walked into a Salon which was larger than the Library and even more beautiful.

The paintings on the walls were all of the previous Duchesses of Oswestry, but Udela's eyes were on the Duke's face as he said:

"I can see you are worried. Tell me what is troubling you."

"It is your . . . brother . . . Lord Julius," Udela replied, the colour rising in her cheeks. "He will know that . . . what we are pretending is not . . . true, and that I came to London . . . yesterday because he . . . told me to."

She expected the Duke to be surprised, but instead he answered:

"I had of course thought of that already. If he questions you, which I have no intention of allowing him to do, the answer is that while you had believed and hoped there was an understanding between us, you thought I would still think you too young to be married."

Udela's eyes were raised to his as he went on:

"You therefore wished to provide for yourself until such time as I intimated that I was ready to have our engagement announced to the world."

Udela drew in her breath and her eyes brightened.

"That is clever of you . . . very clever."

"It is what I would have expected you to think in the circumstances, and I have a feeling that when your father died you would not have written to ask me to come and assist you."

"No, I would not have done that," Udela agreed. "It would have been impossible because I would have been trying to entice you—as your grandmother tells me other . . . women have tried to . . . entice you—into . . . marriage before you were ready for it."

"Are you sure you would have struggled alone?" the Duke asked.

Udela knew that cynically he did not believe that she would not have told him of her predicament. After a moment she said:

"I think if a woman loved a man . . . really loved him . . . she would not wish to . . . capture or catch him . . . or try to keep him a prisoner . . . but would want him to feel free."

"And you think that is what you would feel about the man you love?" the Duke asked.

"I would hope so, but I do know I would never try to force him to love me. Love is something that must be given . . . not taken. Love must be spontaneous and must come from the heart and not the mind."

The Duke looked surprised.

"Who told you to say that?"

"I do not think . . . anybody told me what to think about love . . . it is just what I know instinctively that one should feel . . . and what I have seen."

Now there was no doubt of the scorn in the Duke's voice as he questioned:

"What you have seen? Is there so much love in Little Storton?"

For the first time Udela felt annoyed by his attitude and not so afraid of him as she had been previously.

"What it all comes to, Your Grace, is that people have hearts. My father and mother loved each other deeply, and there were many people in the village, people whom you would think beneath your condescension, but who are nevertheless human beings, capable of deep and true emotions."

She spoke almost hotly, then was surprised at her own daring.

The Duke did not reply and after a moment she said in the humble voice in which she had always spoken to him before:

"Forgive . . . me. I should not have . . . spoken like . . . that. I can only . . . apologise."

"I have no wish for you to apologise," the Duke said. "I think if we are to spend quite a lot of time in each other's company it would be intolerable if either of us did not speak the truth. I am only surprised at your sentiments."

"Why?"

"Because you have obviously considered the subject of love quite seriously and I should have thought you were too young."

Udela smiled.

"Papa said once that women start dreaming about love as soon as they are born . . . but men think it is something rather . . . girlish, until they fall in love."

The Duke laughed.

"Your father was obviously a philosopher."

"I think actually he considered himself to be a student of human nature."

"Is that why he went into the Church?"

"The real reason was that he wanted to get away from his rather overbearing family and his life in

Northumberland. But he was also a sportsman. In fact, they called him 'the Hunting Parson.' "

"So you have been brought up in the field of sport!"

"I used to hunt with Papa when we had the horses," Udela said, "and he started a Cricket Club in the village. We beat all the other villagers round about."

"To get back to the beginning of our conversation—what else did your father say about love?"

"He used to say that if a man was a good sportsman, whatever his class, he would be a good husband."

"And if he was a bad sportsman?"

"He would make his wife unhappy and would bump and bore or even cheat in his own house as easily as he did elsewhere."

The Duke laughed.

"I wish I could have talked to your father."

"He was very amusing and he enjoyed life so much until my mother ... died. Then everything ... changed."

There was a little sob in Udela's voice which was unmistakable, but the Butler announced dinner and it was no longer possible to talk intimately.

Because she was frightened of boring the Duke, she talked to him about his paintings and his horses and the books she had seen in the Library.

"Do you read much?" she asked. "What I enjoyed more than anything else was reading with Papa."

"What did you read?" the Duke asked.

"History and poetry. Papa read Pindar's poems to me in the original Greek."

The Duke raised his eye-brows.

"You are obviously highly educated."

"I would like to think so, but the more one

reads, the more one realises how much there is to learn. Of one thing I know I am very ignorant."

"What is that?"

"Your world, the world I have of course heard about and read about in the newspapers and magazines. It seems very unreal, just as I suppose the way the Senators behaved in Rome seemed unreal then to the ordinary people."

"Are you comparing the frivolities of the Regency with the orgies and licentiousness of Rome at the time of Nero?" the Duke asked.

It was the sort of question he might have asked one of his friends at the Club and would undoubtedly have received a witty if risqué reply.

Udela replied seriously:

"I suppose in every period in history there is a certain stratum of society which is fashionable and, to those who are not part of it, somewhat outrageous, but it is only seen in its proper perspective when we look back on it centuries later."

The Duke thought over what she had said and came to the conclusion that she was right.

"I wonder what the historians will make of us?" he questioned.

"I think they will speak of it," Udela replied, "as a time when if one was rich and important, life could be extremely enjoyable, but for those who were poor, those who had fought on the field of battle, and those who were exploited, it was a time of degradation and misery."

The Duke stiffened and looked at her in sheer astonishment.

"Is that your father's opinion or your own?"

"It is my own, but I have discussed it with my father."

"I suppose you think like that because you were brought up in a Vicarage."

"I hope not," Udela said quickly. "What I would like to do would be to help constructively those who are unfortunate."

"What do you mean—constructively?" the Duke asked sharply.

He thought it exceedingly suspicious that anyone so young and lovely as Udela should be talking about things he did not hear about except from reformers like Wilberforce.

He disliked people who had an exaggerated, almost fanatical desire to change or what they called "reform" everything in the country.

He had never, and this was the truth, discussed such matters with any of the women with whom he usually dined.

Now, as he waited for Udela's reply, he thought, and it was quite unreasonable, that in some way he was being tricked by her.

In her soft, musical voice which made what she was talking about seem strangely inappropriate to her appearance, she was saying:

"I would like there to be new reforms from Parliament and something more inspiring than money given to local authorities to help those who are dependent upon them."

She paused as the Duke did not speak, then went on:

"The County Work-Houses are in most cases horrible places from which a man who is growing old or a woman in ill-health finds it impossible to escape. They cannot work to get out, and even if they do, they have nowhere to go."

"They at least have a roof over their heads," the Duke remarked.

He did not know why he was arguing, but he just felt perverse.

"A human being wants more than that," Udela said. "We want understanding and love."

"So we are back to love," the Duke said. "Are you prepared to provide it for the multitude?"

"They could provide it for themselves, if they had the opportunity," Udela replied quietly. "Families are broken up because they have not enough money to keep them together. And if the breadwinner is injured or taken away to fight in a war, then the home and the family is disbanded, and that is where the trouble begins."

The Duke had no reply and after a moment she said:

"I feel that you understand such things. You could speak about them in the House of Lords and help those who have no idea what ordinary people want."

"Why should you think I am different?" the Duke enquired.

"Because you were kind to me, I know you are a kind person," Udela replied. "Because I sense you are clever and intelligent, there is no need for me to describe to you the state of affairs that exists outside this magnificent house and the parts of London where those who are rich live."

The Duke thought to himself that this was the strangest conversation he had ever had with a woman who looked like Udela.

Aloud he remarked:

"You are making me nervous!"

"Why?"

"Because we have enough crusaders already making trouble for the Government and wanting to spend a great deal of money which the country cannot afford."

Udela did not speak but her eyes rested for a second on the gold candelabrum which lit the ta-

ble and the exquisite gold ornaments which stood
beside the Sèvres dishes which were filled with
muscat grapes and huge peaches such as she had
eaten for breakfast.

She wondered if she had the courage—or was it
the impertinence?—to point out the discrepancies
between him and those whom she was champion-
ing. Then she said a little hesitatingly:

"I am told that His Majesty, when Prince Regent, spent a fortune on the Royal Pavilion at
Brighton, and another on Carlton House."

"You are surely not suggesting that our Monarch
should not be housed as befits his station?"

"No, I am only suggesting that if there is money
for him there should also be money to help those
who cannot help themselves ... like the soldiers
who were ... wounded fighting in ... France, and
the ... sailors who were turned away from their
ships without ... recognition."

These were two subjects on which the Duke had
spoken quite forcefully in the House of Lords.

He had been incensed, as a great many of his
contemporaries had been, by the manner in which
the British Army, having beaten Napoleon at
Waterloo, had been disbanded with what seemed
almost indecent haste, and those who had fought
so valiantly had in the last five years been forgotten or ignored.

Yet he had never at any time discussed such
matters with women, nor had he found one who
was the least interested in anything which did not
concern her personally.

He looked at Udela and found it hard to believe
that she had what he was beginning to suspect was
a sharp, analytical mind.

The servants had left the room, and now, sitting

back with a glass of brandy in his hand, the Duke said with a smile:

"You know, Udela, I am rather worried about you."

"Why?"

"Because I am beginning to think that when our little adventure is over, it will be difficult for me to find you a husband."

Her eyes widened in surprise and she asked:

"Why . . . why should you . . . think that?"

"Because men dislike clever women and most of all they abhor being lectured by them."

Udela gave a little cry.

"Oh . . . please . . . I was not . . . doing that! I was not lecturing you, and it would be a great . . . impertinence for me to . . . attempt to do so."

She looked at him pleadingly before she said:

"You asked me my opinion, so I talked to you as I used to talk to my father. I will . . . try not to do so . . . again."

"But I hope this is the first of many discussions, now that I know where your interests lie," the Duke said. "I was only thinking that it was a strange conversation for me to have with a woman who is as attractive as you. I am certain that most of the eligible suitors for your hand would have been very discomfited."

"You sound, Your Grace, as if you are determined to get me up the aisle."

"It struck me as being the obvious solution to your problem when our engagement is broken."

"Then please . . . forget such . . . ideas."

"Why?"

"For two reasons: One, I have no wish for anyone to arrange my marriage, and I know you will agree with me on that score; and secondly, I would hate to marry into the Social World."

"Of which you know nothing!" the Duke said drily.

"Only what I have read and heard and which, strange though it may seem, is talked about in places like Little Storton."

"You surprise me," the Duke said. "And could they possibly know anything about it?"

Udela smiled and he thought for a moment, although it seemed incredible, that she was laughing at him.

"The servants at Eldridge House," she said, "all take their turn in going to London when His Lordship is in residence there, or else they have relatives working in other houses."

She saw the surprise in the Duke's expression and continued:

"The children and grandchildren of the people on the Eldridge Estate have been employed not only by the late Lord Eldridge but by his relatives and his friends."

She smiled as she went on:

"The Head Forester's daughter is lady's-maid to Her Majesty at Buckingham Palace, while the son of the Butler is a footman at Carlton House."

The Duke put back his head and laughed.

"Now I understand why nothing that happens in London remains a secret for long, in any other part of the country."

"I assure you the gossip in St. James's Street is only twenty-four hours old when it reaches the village," Udela said with a smile.

"That is something I never envisaged," the Duke said. "Now I understand many things that have puzzled and surprised me in the past."

As he spoke, he was thinking that perhaps it was not always the women he favoured who were responsible, as he had imagined, for the gossip which had infuriated him when he was involved with them.

Now he told himself that their lady's-maids, their footmen and their coachmen, and their Chefs and their kitchen-boys had doubtless been all too eager to talk about him, which was why he had often said angrily that it was impossible to keep a secret.

As if she knew what he was thinking, Udela said:

"Papa said once it is not that little pitchers have big ears, but the boy who cleans your shoes has a big mouth!"

She made the Duke laugh, and later in the evening when she was alone in her bedroom she thought that he had in fact laughed quite a lot during the time they had been together.

In fact, when he had bade her good-night he had said:

"Thank you for a very amusing evening, Udela, and if I may say so, an unexpectedly stimulating one."

"I promise not to try to reform Your Grace," she said with a hint of mischief in her eyes.

"You would find it hard to do that," the Duke replied. "At the same time, I am prepared to listen to your ideas, which is more than I can say of the Leaders of the Opposition in the Houses of Parliament!"

"I am very flattered," Udela said in a demure voice, "but I have already realised that some of the subjects about which we talked tonight are on the list of items I must avoid."

"I have not said so," the Duke said quickly.

"I am aware of what you are thinking," Udela replied, "and I promise to be very . . . careful and to be more . . . conventional."

"Not when we are alone," the Duke answered.

"If you were not as stimulating as you were tonight, I am sure I should find it very dull."

"That is actually what I am afraid of being."

"Then your fears are ungrounded, if our conversation at dinner is a sample of what I can expect in your company."

Then he laughed again.

"Go to bed, Udela, and stop making me think when I want to relax. We both of us have quite an ordeal to face tomorrow and we shall need all our wits about us."

Udela drew in her breath.

"I . . . promise I will be very . . . very careful."

She moved towards the door, then stopped.

"Are you also going to bed, Your Grace?"

The Duke shook his head.

"Have you forgotten," he replied, "that this is my last night of freedom?"

He was teasing, but she said:

"As a bachelor there must be a variety of entertainments from which you can choose."

"I am sure there are," he answered, "but I have the uncomfortable feeling that most of them will prove disappointing."

There flashed through her mind what his grandmother had told her about his becoming disillusioned and cynical because of the way in which a woman had treated him.

Impulsively, without thinking, she said:

"One day you will find . . . someone you will . . . love and who will . . . love you just for . . . yourself."

For a moment the Duke was still, then he frowned.

"Why should you say that?" he asked sharply.

Now there was an angry note in his voice which frightened her.

"I am ... sorry," Udela said, and slipped out of the room before he could say any more.

Only as she crossed the Hall and ran up the stairs did she realise that she had made a mistake.

"I must be more careful," she chided herself, "for although he seems very charming ... he can still ... when one least expects it, be ... frightening!"

Chapter Four

Walking into the Library alone, the Duke thought with satisfaction that everything had gone even better than he had anticipated.

His grandmother had insisted that when they sent the note to their relatives in London informing them that his engagement would be in the *Times* that morning, they must hold a small family Reception in the afternoon.

He had groaned at the idea but had agreed to her suggestion, knowing that it was eminently sensible.

As he had expected, everybody who had been invited arrived full of curiosity to see Udela, and, he thought now, they had gone away completely convinced that at last, after they had despaired of it, he had fallen in love.

There had been no doubt that Udela had played to perfection the part he had assigned to her.

Wearing a white gown which made her look very young and very unsophisticated, she had also looked extremely lovely.

His experienced eye was aware that his grandmother had made the very best use of what was really raw material and had turned it into something so polished, so exquisite, that it would have been difficult for even the most carping critic to find fault.

With her fair hair dressed in the very latest fashion, with a little powder on her clear, unblemished skin, and with a touch of salve on her lips as was the fashion, Udela captivated his Westry relations and he knew their approval would be carried all over London by the evening.

The Duke had told Udela before the Reception to answer as few questions as possible.

"You will be bombarded with them," he said, "and the easiest thing for you to do is to wait for me to reply, and to look pretty but stupid."

"I am sure I can do that very competently," Udela had answered.

She spoke humbly and sincerely, and the Duke, after a sharp glance at her to see that she was not offended by his suggestion, said:

"After our conversation last night, I am perfectly prepared to compliment you on your intelligence, but not when my relatives are listening."

They had been alone for just a few minutes after luncheon, and, looking over her shoulder to see that no one could hear, she said in a very low voice:

"If Lord Julius ... comes to the party ... what am I to ... do?"

"I would not mind wagering a very substantial sum that he will not appear," the Duke said. "But if he does, leave him to me."

"But ... what shall I ... say? What ... shall I do?"

"Nothing," he said firmly. "I have thought this over carefully, Udela, and I am sure that just as we pretend to ourselves you were not met at Islington by my brother's carriage, so we pretend you have never met him."

"Never met him?" Udela repeated.

"No!" the Duke said firmly. "And I think, bad though he is, he has some sense of shame and will not press that previous occasion upon you, now that he realises that you are betrothed to me."

Udela looked doubtful and a little frightened, but, because she did not wish to argue with the Duke, she said no more.

As the guests were announced one after the other and came into the huge elegant Salon which stretched the whole length of the first floor, she was tense and afraid that Lord Julius would be amongst them.

It was comforting to know that the Duke was standing beside her and that he was very large, strong, and, she told herself, protective.

It would have been unnatural if she had not been aware before she left her bedroom that she looked very different from the badly dressed girl whom Lord Julius had seen carrying flowers to the Church-yard.

"It would be difficult for him to recognise me," she told her reflection in the mirror.

She thought that in fact even her father might have some difficulty if he could see her now.

Before the Duchess had started to order her clothes, Udela had said a little hesitatingly:

"I suppose . . . Ma'am . . . I really ought to wear . . . black or grey . . . because I am in . . . mourning."

As she spoke, she thought that the Duke might think it too sombre and unattractive for the part he wished her to play, and as the Duchess frowned, she added quickly:

"But . . . unless you think it wrong, I need not

wear it ... because Papa always disapproved of ... mourning."

"He did?" the Duchess questioned with raised eye-brows. "I thought he was a Parson."

"He was, but rather an unusual one," Udela replied, "and he said that since we are Christians we mourn only for ourselves, not for the person who has gone to God."

"That is an extremely sensible attitude," the Duchess said. "I have always thought excessive mourning was unnecessary."

There was a faint smile on her lips as she added as cynically as her grandson might have spoken:

"The widows who lost their husbands in the war may have worn black, but a large number of them showed no sign of mourning in their private lives."

Udela did not know that the Duchess was in fact referring to the outrageous way in which Lady Marlene had behaved after her husband had died of his war wounds.

She had been afraid that because Lady Marlene was so beautiful, her grandson would fall captive to her attractions and would marry her.

It was a relief that she could not express, to find that unexpectedly he had chosen a girl as sweet and unspoilt as Udela.

Privately, however, she wondered if Udela would be able to make the Duke happy and wean him away from his numerous love-affairs.

The Duke would have been astonished and extremely annoyed if he had been aware that the majority of his relations, including his grandmother, were cognisant of his affairs almost from the moment they started.

He had no idea now, for instance, that his grandmother had been told some hours ago by her lady's-maid, who had been told by the Butler, who had been informed by the footman, that a note had arrived for him from Mrs. Elsie Shannon.

It was lying where his secretary had left it on the blotter on his desk, which was where he habitually found the private letters which Mr. Humphries was wise enough to know were not intended for any eyes but his.

As the Duke crossed the room and saw the letter lying there, he was for a moment apprehensive in case it was from Lady Marlene.

Then when he was near enough to see the handwriting, his expression changed. He sat down and, with a little smile on his face, picked up his gold letter-opener with its jewelled handle.

He drew open the letter, but there was an expression in his eyes which would have told an observer that he was not certain of what he would read.

Mrs. Shannon, however, was very different from Lady Marlene.

If she had been piqued or angry at reading of the Duke's engagement in the *Gazette,* she was far too clever to say so.

Instead, she had written the Duke a warm letter of congratulations, wishing him every happiness. It was only the last paragraph which was revealing:

I know how busy you will be, Randolph, and I would not, of course, encroach on your time with your fiancée, but if you have a moment to spare, it would be such a pleasure to give you my congratulations personally, and to offer you, as ever, my friendship and love.

The Duke sat back in his chair and decided that he would certainly have a few minutes to call on Elsie Shannon.

He had found her extremely attractive after he

had finished with Lady Marlene, and although she was by no means as beautiful, she had other qualities which the Duke found immeasurably more enjoyable.

These included a calm temperament, and, perhaps most important of all, she possessed a husband.

Never again, the Duke had sworn to himself, would he have an affair with a woman whose one object was to trap him into giving her a wedding-ring.

Colonel Shannon, who was many years older than his wife, was an extremely successful race-horse owner. He disliked London and preferred to spend his time at Newmarket or anywhere else in the country where his horses were racing.

He gave his wife money and a liberty that was the envy of a large number of other wives whose husbands were not so accommodating.

Elsie Shannon had been about London for a number of years. She was nearly as old as the Duke and almost as experienced with men as he was with women.

He found that she amused him and filled a place in his life at a moment when Lady Marlene had annoyed and irritated him to the point where he told himself he was sick to death of women, and that included all of them.

'I might have guessed Elsie would behave properly,' he thought as he unlocked a drawer for which only he had a key and put her letter in it.

He was just wondering whether, as he had an hour to spare before he need dress for dinner, he would look in at White's to see what reaction there had been to the announcement of his engagement, when the Library door opened and the Butler announced:

"Lord Julius Westry, Your Grace!"

The Duke turned his head slowly, thinking, as he did so, how much he disliked his brother and how, although he had expected to see him, he had hoped it would not be this evening.

Lord Julius walked towards the desk and stood looking at his brother aggressively.

"I have come," he said, "as you might have expected, to collect something which belongs to me and which you mistakenly brought in from the streets the night before last."

The Duke looked at him in surprise.

"I do not know what you are talking about!"

"You know perfectly well," Lord Julius replied in a rude voice. "The 'bit o' muslin' I collected from the country was allowed by my damn-fool servants to run away from the place to which they were taking her, and I assume she appealed to your sense of chivalry."

He almost spat the words at the Duke, who was still staring at him.

Then as his brother did not speak Lord Julius said:

"Come on, Randolph, we are not going to play games with each other. The woman is mine, so, as you have plenty of love-birds of your own, hand her over. I suppose she is hidden somewhere in this Mausoleum."

Slowly, because it seemed almost impossible to speak, the Duke said:

"I was expecting you, Julius, but I imagined that the reason for your visit was to congratulate me."

"What on?"

The Duke looked at him searchingly for a long moment, then at length he questioned:

"You have not seen the *Gazette* today?"

"No," his brother replied. "As a matter of fact, I was out of London. What have I missed?"

"What you have missed," the Duke said quietly, "is the announcement of my engagement."

For a moment there was complete silence. Then Lord Julius, in a voice that sounded strange even to himself, ejaculated:

"Did you say—your engagement?"

"It is in the *Gazette*," the Duke replied. "I thought surely someone would have informed you of such a momentous occasion."

"I thought one or two people were looking at me strangely," Lord Julius said almost to himself.

Then as if he could not believe what he had heard, he said:

"It cannot be true! You have always said you would never marry!"

"I have changed my mind."

"Then you have no right to do so. I am your heir! You have made it abundantly clear not only to me but to everybody else that you intended to remain a bachelor."

"As one grows older, one sees the error of one's ways," the Duke said lightly.

"But you cannot do this!" Lord Julius said, and now he was shouting. "Change your mind, indeed! And what am I to do? I am your heir-presumptive."

"You are, I think, the only one of my relatives who did not plead with me, beg me, and almost order me to take a wife," the Duke said. "Well, I have done what was expected of me, and I can assure you that everyone, including Grandmama, is delighted!"

"They would be!" Lord Julius retorted. "They have always hated me! They have always been determined that while you had everything, I should have nothing!"

"I hardly think that is a fair statement," the Duke replied. "In the last five years I have paid your debts half-a-dozen times, and you have an exceedingly generous allowance."

"Your idea of generous and mine are different," Lord Julius said, sneering. "Who is this damned girl who you intend to make your wife?"

The words sounded almost like the hiss of a serpent.

"She is the granddaughter of Major-General Sir Alexander Massingburgh," the Duke answered, "of whom you must have heard. But otherwise she is new to London."

Lord Julius, however, was not listening. He had walked across to the window to stand staring with unseeing eyes at the flower-filled garden.

"Why should you do this to me?" he asked. "Why should you suddenly change your way of life after everybody was certain that you would pass the title on to me?"

"It must be a disappointment for you," the Duke said, "but I suppose every man wants a son, sooner or later, to follow him."

"So that is what you are looking for!" Lord Julius exclaimed.

He spoke quietly, then suddenly he turned round and his face was contorted.

"I will not have it—do you hear? I will not allow you to do this! You shall not take the title from me!"

His voice seemed to echo round the room, and the Duke, with an expression of distaste on his face, said:

"Behave yourself, Julius! The servants will hear you."

"Do you think I care what they hear?" Lord Julius stormed. "I expect they will be laughing—

laughing to think you have disinherited me, thrown me back into the gutter where you have always wished me to be."

The Duke sighed.

"These ridiculous accusations are untrue, Julius, as you are well aware. Would you like to know exactly what your bills totalled the last time I paid them?"

"I am not interested in bills!" Lord Julius screamed. "I want to be the Duke of Oswestry, and by God, that is what I will be, if I have to kill you for it!"

The Duke rose to his feet.

"Go away, Julius, and stop making a fool of yourself," he said sternly. "If you talk like this, people will think you are deranged, and I am beginning to think so myself."

"That is what you would like, would you not?" Lord Julius sneered. "To shut me up in Bedlam and be rid of me. Well, I can promise you, you will regret the day you tried to trick me out of what is mine by right!"

He was still screaming at the top of his voice as the Duke walked across the room to the grog-tray.

"Let me give you a drink, Julius," he said. "There is no use in our discussing this any further."

He poured out a glass of champagne and carried it across the room to his brother, who was standing with his back to the window, his face contorted to such an extent that he looked like a gargoyle.

The Duke held the glass out to him, but Lord Julius with a swift movement struck it from his hand so that it fell to the floor and smashed, the champagne leaving a wet patch on the carpet.

"Go to the devil!" he said. "And I hope you and your offspring rot in hell!"

He walked towards the door, then as he reached it he stopped.

"As you are to be married, or you think you are," he said, "you will not need the 'bit o' muslin' who sought your protection the night before last. I daresay now that you have handled her she will not be worth the money I expected to get for her, but I will take her with me nevertheless."

"I have not the least idea what you are talking about," the Duke said. "The only lady who arrived here the night before last was my future wife, Miss Udela Hayward!"

The astonishment on Lord Julius's face was ludicrous to behold.

It seemed as if he was about to burst into another tirade against the Duke. Then he changed his mind.

His eyes narrowed until they were mere slits on either side of his long nose, and his thin lips were a sharp line across his face.

Then with a sound of sheer, unmitigated fury he pulled open the door and passed through it, slamming it behind him.

The Duke stood for a long moment listening to hear that he had actually gone. Then he walked across the room to pour himself a drink.

When he had done so, he carried it in his hand across to the window.

As he did so, he was thinking that while he had expected Julius to take the announcement of his marriage badly, his brother's reaction had in fact exceeded his expectations.

His threats were of course farcical. At the same time, the Duke had the uncomfortable feeling that if it was possible for him to make trouble, he would do so.

He had already realised that Julius would no

longer find it easy to borrow money from Usurers on his expectations.

The Duke was well aware that Usurers eventually extorted astronomical sums for the loan of what had at the beginning been quite a small sum.

He had paid Julius's debts over and over again, and he thought it was not fair to his other relatives who frequently looked to him for help, nor to the Estates themselves, that he should go on paying out so much to one member of the family.

He had always known that his brother was jealous of him and hated his own position as second son, but he had never known until now that Julius was almost fanatical on the subject.

How could he have imagined that he would behave as a complete outsider? No gentleman of any breeding would take any girl like Udela to a bawdy-house.

"What am I to do," the Duke asked himself, "to prevent Julius from behaving so abominably?"

He knew that his friends must be aware of his brother's activities, and out of consideration of his feelings they had not informed him who was financing Mrs. Crawley.

It was humiliating enough to think that a Westry could go round the country collecting girls for her nefarious trade, and it was something, the Duke told himself, that he himself could not connive at.

However, he was not quite certain how he could stop it. He was sure Mrs. Crawley and Julius were making large sums of money and were doubtless breaking a number of laws.

But he could not inform on his own brother, nor did he wish to face a scandal involving a Westry being taken to the Old Bailey.

'There must be something I can do,' he thought despairingly.

He tried to tell himself that when Julius had got over his rage at the idea of his being married, they could perhaps have a quiet talk and he could offer him money, on condition that he would behave better and first and foremost would sever his connection with the house on Hay Hill.

Although he tried to deny it, the Duke felt upset and on edge after the scene which had just ensued.

He suddenly thought he had had enough of his family for one day. It had been an effort to be pleasant to his aunts and uncles and the innumerable cousins who had attended the Reception.

He had always thought they were a dull and tiresome collection and decided that en masse they depressed him.

Now, after Julius's behaviour, he thought that he could not bear to talk about the Westrys or about his marriage and that where that was concerned, he had done enough for the day.

He rang the bell, and when the servant came he told him to fetch his Comptroller.

Only a few minutes later Mr. Humphries came into the room.

"You wanted me, Your Grace?"

He was a distinguished-looking man with grey hair who had served in the Duke's Regiment at the beginning of the century but had been too old to take part in the Battle of Waterloo.

"Yes, Humphries," the Duke said. "I want you to inform my grandmother that I have been called away and unfortunately cannot give myself the pleasure of dining with her and Miss Hayward this evening."

"I will inform Her Grace."

"I want a groom to take this note to Mrs. Shannon's house and await her answer."

The Duke, while he had been waiting, had scribbled a few words on a piece of paper and sealed the envelope.

He now handed this to Mr. Humphries, who looked impassively at the Duke and said quietly:

"A groom will leave immediately."

"Thank you, Humphries. I suppose you are aware that Lord Julius called on me just now?"

"I was told he had done so, Your Grace."

"I suppose you are also aware of what devilment he is up to now?"

The Duke saw by the expression in his Comptroller's eyes that, as usual in anything that affected his well-being, Mr. Humphries was aware of it almost before he was himself.

"I had heard certain disquieting rumours, Your Grace."

"Very disquieting!" the Duke said. "What are we to do about it?"

"I imagine that to stop it you will have to pay out."

"That is what I thought myself."

"It will be expensive. Mrs. Crawley has become the fashion, I am told."

"You have heard correctly," the Duke said bitterly. "But can I afford to go on bleeding the Estate for Julius? You know as well as I do that he is insatiable where money is concerned."

"The question is, Your Grace, whether you can afford not to," Mr. Humphries said quietly.

The Duke did not reply and after a moment's silence Mr. Humphries added:

"I will send this note as you requested, Your Grace," and went from the room.

* * *

Upstairs, the Duchess, who had changed into a comfortable negligé, was talking to Udela.

"You were a great success this afternoon, my dear," she said, "and everyone congratulated me on Randolph's future wife."

She gave Udela a very sweet smile before she added:

"We have always been afraid, desperately afraid, that he would marry somebody unsuitable, or, worse still, refuse, as he has done for so many years, to marry anyone."

"So many, many ladies must have wanted to marry him," Udela said.

She found it very hard when the Duchess talked to her intimately and with such charm not to tell her the truth, not to confess that she and the Duke were acting a lie and that he did in fact intend to remain unmarried as they all feared.

She knew, however, that her loyalty lay towards the man who had protected her. Nevertheless, even in the short time she had been at Oswestry House, she had an affection for the Duchess because in some ways she reminded her of her mother.

It was perhaps because the Dowager always found something kind and nice to say about everybody. Moreover, she had a fondness for her grandson that showed itself not only in words but in the expression on her face whenever he was present.

Udela felt she could feel the love the Duchess poured out towards him.

"I suppose," the Duchess said now, "every woman has favourites in her life, and mine has always been Randolph. He was such an adorable small boy, so handsome and so loving, and he crept into my heart almost the moment he was born."

She paused for a moment before she continued:

"I pray every night that I will not die before I can hold Randolph's son in my arms, and that is another reason why I feel so happy today."

Udela clenched her fingers together because she was afraid she might say something which would take the happiness from the Duchess's face.

Wishing to change the subject, she said:

"You have . . . another grandson . . . but he did not . . . come today."

"I did not ask him," the Duchess replied. "I do not want to say anything to prejudice you against the Westrys, but I suppose there is always a black sheep in every family."

"And Lord Julius is one?"

"I am afraid so," the Duchess answered. "He was always a difficult child, and he was sent away from several Schools which refused to keep him."

"That must have been very upsetting for you and for His Grace's mother and father."

"I think they broke their hearts over Julius," the Duchess replied, "and no one could have done more for him than his brother. But he is hopeless —quite hopeless."

As if she did not wish to go on talking of her grandson, she said:

"Tomorrow I am to take you to meet some dear friends of mine, and after that I understand that Randolph wishes us to go to the country."

"To the country?" Udela asked eagerly.

"Yes. I think it is a mistake to leave London so soon, especially as so few of your clothes are ready, but I suppose he wants to show you the family mansion and I cannot blame him for that."

"No, indeed, Ma'am. It will be very exciting!"

"But perhaps we will not stay long," the Duchess said hopefully. "There will be so many people

you should meet in London. But when Randolph
has made up his mind, you will find there is nothing that will change it."

Udela did not reply to the Duchess, but she
knew she had no wish to change the Duke's mind.

It had been very frightening to meet his relations,
and although they had all been charming, she was
still aware that at the back of her mind was always
the knowledge that Lord Julius had yet to appear.

When he did, what would he say? Would he de-
nounce her as the girl he had brought to London
for a very different purpose?

And was the Duke right in saying that there was
nothing Lord Julius could do?

She had no answers to these questions.

All she wanted was to put as much distance between herself and Lord Julius as possible, and she
felt that when she reached the country she need no
longer be so afraid of him.

The Duchess intended to rest for an hour before
dinner and told Udela she should do the same
thing.

Obediently Udela went to her own bedroom, but
when she reached it she thought that she was not in
the least tired and if she was to lie down she did
not want to sleep but to read.

She had seen when she had been in the Library
that the newspapers were all arranged on a long,
low stool in front of the fire.

If the Duke did not require them, she wondered
if she could read, as she had always done at home,
the Parliamentary reports which had interested her
father.

She also wanted, although she had been too shy
to say so, to see the announcement of her and the
Duke's engagement in the *Gazette*.

She started down the stairs, saying to herself as she went:

"While I am in the Library I will choose a book to read. I am sure the Duke has the latest novel of Sir Walter Scott and perhaps a recent volume of Lord Byron's poems."

She and her father had been extravagant when it came to books, but on his death she had known that she dare not spend money unnecessarily.

She must not only pay their debts but conserve everything she could for her own future.

When she reached the Hall she saw that there was a footman in attendance.

"Is His Grace in the Library?" she asked.

"His Grace has gone upstairs to change, Miss," the footman replied. "I think he is dining out."

Udela felt a little pang of disappointment. She had thought of dining with the Duke and talking with him as she had done last night.

Then she told herself that if she was to be alone, there was all the more reason for her to have something to read.

Aloud she said to the footman:

"I want to choose a book in the Library."

He hurried across the Hall to open the door for her, and as she entered the room, she saw, as she had expected, the newspapers lying on the stool on the hearth-rug.

She picked up the *Times* and the *Morning Post,* then put them down again while she went to the bookcase.

She had not been mistaken. There were the Walter Scott novels, which all the world knew the Prince Regent enjoyed, bound in the most expensive Russian leather.

Udela selected two that she had not yet read, then put them down and looked along the shelves and in another bookcase until she found Lord Byron's poems.

There were a great number of other poets on the same shelf and she pulled out the books one after another, knowing that they would be a delight to read and wondering which she should choose first.

She found herself thinking that she could only hope that her pretence engagement to the Duke would not be over too quickly, if only so that she could improve her mind and enjoy his Library.

'I wonder if he has the same number of books in the country,' she thought, and opened a book of Shelley's poems that she had never seen before.

She was so intent on what she was reading that she did not hear the door of the Library open, then she heard a servant say:

"I'll tell His Grace you are here, M'Lady!"

Udela raised her head and saw moving into the room the most beautiful woman she had ever seen in her life.

She had never imagined it possible for anyone to be so lovely and at the same time so spectacular.

Wearing a gown that revealed the exquisite lines of her figure and a bonnet that seemed exaggeratedly flamboyant, the newcomer's red hair and slanting green eyes were as sensational as her whole appearance.

"Who are you?"

Her voice was sharp and made Udela aware that she was staring in what was obviously a rude manner.

Quickly she put down the book of poems and curtsyed.

"I am Udela Hayward," she replied.

"So it is you I have to thank for interfering in my life!" the newcomer said sharply.

She saw the surprise in Udela's expression and said:

"As you obviously do not know who I am, let me inform you that my name is Lady Marlene Kelston, and the man you expect to be your husband has behaved in the most treacherous and despicable manner towards me."

Udela was bewildered not only by what Lady Marlene said but by the way she spoke.

There was no beauty in her spiteful voice and even the loveliness of her face seemed for the moment to be contorted.

"I . . . am . . . sorry," she said hesitatingly.

"Sorry? What are you sorry for? I suppose you think you are clever in catching him when so many other women have failed. But let me tell you, he will betray you as he has betrayed so many others, and break your heart if you have the least fondness for him."

Again Lady Marlene was speaking with a spite and a vindictiveness that made Udela wince.

"I . . . am sorry," she said again, "b-but I think . . . perhaps you should say these things to . . . His Grace . . . not to . . . me."

"He can listen too, for all I care," Lady Marlene retorted. "Perhaps it will do you good to know what sort of man you contemplate marrying. A Judas, a man who is not even prepared to be responsible for the child he has fathered!"

Udela looked towards the door. It seemed a long way away, and yet she knew it was a mistake for her to stay here listening to this beautiful woman while she defamed the Duke.

She thought that perhaps this explained why he needed her help now.

Even as she thought of him, the door opened and the Duke came in.

He had already changed into evening-dress, but Udela had only to glance at his face to know that he was angry.

"What are you doing here, Marlene?" he enquired.

"You were not expecting me?" she asked. "What a surprise!"

She was being sarcastic, and the Duke looked at Udela.

"My grandmother requires you upstairs, Udela."

"No. Let her stay," Lady Marlene interposed. "It will do her good to learn what sort of husband she will have. If she has any high-flown ideas about you, she might as well be disillusioned sooner than later."

Udela was walking, as the Duke had told her, towards the door. She had almost reached it when Lady Marlene said to her:

"Stay here! It will do you good to hear the truth."

Udela looked uncertainly at the Duke.

"Go to my grandmother," he said quietly, but there was no doubt that it was a command she must obey.

Only as she went out into the Hall did she hear Lady Marlene laugh before she said:

"If you really think that little milk-sop can keep you amused for more than ten minutes, you must be crazy!"

There was so much scorn in her tone that Udela felt almost as if Lady Marlene had used a whip against her.

Then, because her heart was beating quickly, her mouth felt dry, and once again she was afraid, she ran across the Hall and up the stairs to her own room!

* * *

In the Library the Duke faced Lady Marlene with an expression on his face which stifled the words she was about to say.

"If you came here to make a scene, Marlene," he said, "then you have succeeded. I now request you to leave, and if you do not do so, I shall order the servants to see you out."

"Can you really speak to me like that?" she asked.

"You are behaving, as you are well aware, like a fish-wife. While you have contrived to make yourself singularly unpleasant to a young girl who I imagine has never met a woman like you before, you do not intimidate me, nor do I intend to listen to anything you have to say!"

"I will make you listen!"

"I doubt it," the Duke replied. "Are you leaving quietly, or must I throw you out?"

"You would not dare!"

Lady Marlene snarled the words at him.

"If you do not leave immediately," he replied, "I shall inform my household that you are never to be admitted again and I shall tell my grandmother the reason for your exclusion."

"Your grandmother?"

"She is here to chaperone my future wife," the Duke said. "You have tried to blackmail me with your relations, Marlene, and therefore I am prepared to use mine."

He knew as he spoke that he had used a trump card.

Everyone in the *Beau Monde* knew of the Duchess's social significance. The power she had experienced when her husband was alive had not diminished over the years.

Because the Duke had no wife, the Duchess often acted as hostess for him in the country and sometimes, although less frequently, in London.

There was no one who did not acknowledge that it was not only her position socially which counted, but her personality and character that were admired by everyone from the Prime Minister to every Statesman of any importance.

He knew he had scored a point, and he did not wait for Lady Marlene to reply but opened the door.

As he did so, he said in a voice that could be heard by the servants waiting by the front door:

"Let me escort you to your carriage, and I promise I will tell my grandmother that you called on her. She will be so sorry, as she is resting, not to have been able to see you."

Lady Marlene was defeated and she knew it. At the same time, as she held out her hand to the Duke she said:

"I shall see you again, Randolph. You may be sure of that!"

He bowed over her hand in so perfunctory a manner that it was almost insulting. Then as he did not reply, Lady Marlene turned away angrily and went down the steps to where her carriage was waiting.

Only when she had driven away did the Duke wonder if he should seek out Udela and apologise to her.

Then he told himself that there was nothing he could say that would not be embarrassing, and there was no reason why she should be perturbed or upset.

It was not as though she was fond of him or as if she was in reality his fiancée, in which case Lady Marlene would have created exactly the type of uncomfortable situation she had desired.

What was really important was that she believed he was really engaged to be married.

'I have fooled her as I have fooled all the others,' the Duke told himself with satisfaction.

Then as the closed carriage he used in the evenings came to the door, a footman put his cloak over his shoulders, another handed him his hat, and a third proffered his cane.

It was with a feeling of escape that the Duke drove away towards Mrs. Shannon's house, having already been assured in a note he had received earlier that she was waiting for him with an inexpressible delight.

Chapter Five

The Duke knew that Udela had been shocked by Lady Marlene.

He was aware of the stricken look in her eyes as she had obeyed his orders and left the Library, and as he drove away from Oswestry House he found himself thinking it was deplorable that she had come in contact with anything so unsavoury.

Then he told himself that he was being ridiculous.

His love-affairs were nothing to do with Udela, and if women as debased as Lady Marlene wished to make untrue accusations against him, he had no intention of justifying himself in Udela's or anybody else's eyes.

After all, he had saved her from what she undoubtedly would believe was "a fate worse than death," and her gratitude should include a forgiveness, or anyway a lack of criticism, of his "sins."

Nevertheless, to his own irritation, the thought of Udela persisted the whole evening.

In some extraordinary fashion her face imposed itself on his thoughts in a way which made it difficult to concentrate on what the alluring Mrs. Shannon was saying, and when dinner was over the Duke rose to his feet.

"Must you go, dearest Randolph?" Elsie Shannon asked in surprise. "You have been here such a short time, and I was so looking forward to our being—together."

He was well aware exactly what she meant by the word "together," but unexpectedly he had no wish to make love to her at this particular moment.

As he drove away, knowing he had left her disappointed and frustrated, he told himself that Julius and Lady Marlene were to blame for his unaccountable mood.

But when, after playing cards for very high stakes at White's, he finally got to bed, Udela's unhappy, shocked eyes still disturbed him.

After they reached Oswestry House the next day, he realised how deeply Lady Marlene's visit had perturbed her and he knew that she was avoiding him.

It was strange and very unlike him, but almost unconsciously he had looked for the glint of excitement in her eyes when he talked to her, the shy little glance she would give him if she thought she had said or done something wrong, and the expression of delight which swept across her face when he complimented or congratulated her.

"She is too sensitive and too vulnerable to be anything but a nuisance," he told himself, and was aware that he lied.

Oswestry House in Kent, which was a magnificent example of a Palladian building and had been completed by his grandfather in 1750, was looking, the Duke thought, even more magnificent than usual.

The lush greenery of the trees which made a background for it, the lawns smooth as green velvet, and the flowers that were brilliant patches of colour were a perfect setting for the wings which flanked the lofty, colonnaded central part of the building.

"It is lovely! Magnificent!" he heard Udela say, but she was speaking to the Duchess and not to him.

"I feel the same way every time I come home," his grandmother answered.

"I see I shall have to take you on a tour of the house and tell you the history of its contents," the Duke said to Udela.

"Thank you," she replied dutifully, but she did not look at him as she spoke.

They arrived in the afternoon, and later when the Duke thought he would like to talk to Udela and show her the paintings he was told that she was resting.

When dinner was over and the Duchess said she wished to retire to bed, Udela said she would go with her.

Ordinarily, the Duke knew, her attitude would not have perturbed him in the slightest, except that such behaviour would have been unusual in his experience.

Any woman in whom he had ever shown the slightest interest had made it very clear that her only desire was to be with him, and it had invariably been the case of his avoiding them rather than the other way round.

"Dammit!" he said to himself. "If that is what she wants, I am free, as I have always wanted to be, to enjoy myself in my own way. After all, we have no audience to play to at this particular moment."

However, he spoke too soon, for neighbours arrived to offer their congratulations quite early the morning after they had reached Oswestry House.

Some had come quite a distance and the Duke

was obliged to ask them to stay for luncheon, an invitation they accepted with alacrity.

Then once again, whether she liked it or not, Udela had to play the part of a girl who, having caught the most elusive bachelor in England, was obviously very much in love with him.

She acted the role perfectly, and only the Duke was aware that while her face was turned towards him as she listened to everything he had to say, her eyes never met his.

The visitors left, saying the most complimentary things both to the Duke and the Duchess, and as they drove down the drive their place was taken by other visitors, their numbers increasing hour after hour as the afternoon passed.

"I thought we came here to be quiet and away from the Social World," the Duke complained angrily to his grandmother.

They were alone for a few minutes in the magnificent Salon where the walls were covered with superlative paintings and the furniture would have graced a Royal Palace.

"I know, dearest, but of course it is such an excitement that you have become engaged, and our friends are insatiably curious about Udela."

"Perhaps she should sit on a platform on the lawn and they could all come and stare at her at the same time!" the Duke retorted.

"Are you suggesting we should give a Garden-Party?" the Duchess enquired.

"God forbid!" he replied. "I am only finding it extremely boring to answer the same questions over and over again."

"I am sure it will be better tomorrow," the Duchess said consolingly. "After all, there cannot be many people left to visit us."

"I sincerely hope not!" the Duke replied.

He walked from the Salon and Udela looked at the Duchess in consternation.

"He is . . . angry!"

"Not really," the Duchess replied, "and I can assure you, knowing my grandson as I do, that he would have been very piqued if no one had taken the slightest interest in his marriage."

"Is that true?" Udela asked.

"Randolph is very aware of his own consequence, and although he complains, he knows that the people are as interested in him as they would be if the King could take another wife."

Udela gave a little laugh.

"At least he is better-looking!"

"That is true," the Duchess agreed. "His Majesty has become so fat that he now dislikes being seen by the ordinary public."

Udela, because she was interested, was just going to ask the Duchess more about King George when the Duke came back into the Salon.

"Another carriage has just arrived at the front door," he said. "We must fix the same smile on our lips and listen to the same platitudes as if they were as intelligent as the words of Socrates."

He looked at Udela as he spoke, knowing she would be aware that he was referring to the intelligent conversation they had had the first night they had dined together.

Once again her eyes were not on him but were looking down at the floor, and the Duke was scowling as their new guests were announced.

Because he was determined that the situation between them should not continue, he waited until the Duchess said as they left the Dining-Room after dinner:

"It has been a very long day. I have enjoyed it,

but I am getting old and I find the chatter of voices more tiresome than driving."

"I agree with you," the Duke remarked.

"Then you will understand," the Duchess said, "why what I long for at this moment is my own bed. Good-night, dear boy."

She kissed the Duke and would have kissed Udela but she said quickly:

"I will come with you, Ma'am."

"We will both escort you to the bottom of the stairs," the Duke said firmly, "but I want to talk to Udela for a short while."

As he spoke, he knew that she contemplated making an excuse to go upstairs with the Duchess.

Then, as if she was too frightened to oppose him, as the Duchess started to climb the beautiful gilded staircase, she followed the Duke back into the Salon.

She walked demurely across the room and he thought how graceful she looked in her white gown with its small puffed sleeves of white lace and with the same lace also decorating the wide skirt.

The fashions in the post-war years were far more elaborate than what had been worn during the years of war.

However, the high bodice still held its own, and Udela's figure had a perfection which the Duke thought he had seldom seen on anyone who also had such a beautiful face.

He had found in his long experience of women that any who had one outstanding attribute often lost points on another.

Lady Marlene, for instance, although she had one of the most beautiful faces he had ever seen, had thick ankles which fortunately seldom were visible except to her lovers.

Mrs. Shannon had a perfectly proportioned figure, but she was not really beautiful and she lacked the grace which was very evident where Udela was concerned.

He had not yet discovered a flaw in Udela's beauty, but then, as he told himself, he had not been looking at her particularly intimately.

He was, he was quite certain in his own mind, seeking her out now not in his own interest but in hers.

If they were to live in the same house, it was ridiculous for her to put up a barrier between them of which he was very conscious.

It was because she was so young and so unsophisticated, and also, he thought, because she was a Parson's daughter, that she was inevitably more critical of the loose morals of the Regency than someone who had lived in a different environment.

Udela walked to one of the long windows, and because it was still light and the brilliant colours of the sunset could be seen behind the great trees in the Park, the curtains were not yet drawn.

Overhead, the sky had that translucent beauty which comes before the first stars appear, and the only sound was the caw-caw of the rooks going to roost.

The Duke came to stand beside Udela and although she did not move he had the strange feeling that she had no wish for him to be too near or to touch her.

It was something he had never known a woman to feel before, and after a moment he said:

"I think, Udela, you are being unfair and, if I may say so, unjust."

"What . . . do you . . . mean?" she asked. "H-how can I be . . . either of those things?"

"You are condemning me unheard," he replied.

"Every criminal has the chance to put his own case before the Judge."

She made no pretence of not knowing what he was talking about.

"I would not ... presume to ... judge you ... My Lord."

"But you are condemning me," the Duke insisted.

There was silence for a moment, then Udela said in a very small voice:

"I do not ... think that is what I ... f-feel."

"Then what is it?" the Duke asked.

For a moment he thought she would not reply. Then, as if he compelled her to do so, she said hesitatingly:

"Because you ... live in such ... beautiful surroundings ... because everything about you ... is fine and ... magnificent ... I did not wish to think that you would do ... anything that was ... wrong."

The Duke was too surprised for the moment to reply, and she went on:

"It is like seeing a lovely picture that has been ... damaged, and although I know it is ... none of my business ... I cannot help it ... upsetting me."

The Duke found his voice.

"That is exactly what I would expect you to feel, Udela, if the allegations Lady Marlene made against me were true."

She turned her head quickly and for the first time since they had left London her eyes met his.

"They are ... not true?"

She barely breathed the words.

"I swear to you by everything that I hold sacred," the Duke said quietly, "that Lady Marlene was lying to you."

He thought for a moment that the sunset was reflected in Udela's eyes. Then she said:

"Then . . . why . . . why should she say . . . such a . . . wicked thing? I cannot . . . understand."

"The reason is not far to find," the Duke replied. "I hold a high social position and I am also a wealthy man."

"You . . . mean . . . she wanted your . . . money!"

"Of course!" the Duke replied cynically. "Do women ever want anything else? And whether they expect cash or a wedding-ring, it is still a payment they exact to the last farthing!"

Udela gave a little cry.

"That is not true! There may be some women like that, but not all, and love which is . . . sold is not . . . love . . . as we have said . . . before."

There was still a cynical twist to the Duke's lips, but Udela's voice was pleading and penitent as she said:

"Please . . . forgive me' for thinking that you would . . . behave in any way that was not . . . noble. I see now it was . . . foolish of me to believe anyone who could say such terrible things to a stranger . . . but she was so . . . beautiful."

"I am sure your father would have said one should not judge people by their appearance."

"Papa would be ashamed of me for not trusting my . . . instinct where . . . you are . . . concerned. I should have known after you have been so . . . kind to me that you could . . . never do anything so . . . cruel and unkind as the lady . . . suggested."

There was silence for a moment, then Udela asked:

"What will . . . become of her now?"

"Does that matter to you?" the Duke asked.

"I was not thinking so much about her . . . as of the . . . child."

"You need not worry on that score. Lady Marlene is perfectly capable of looking after herself and her own interests. If I will not marry her, which I have no intention of doing, then she will find some fool to offer for her, even perhaps the man who is actually responsible for her condition."

As the Duke spoke he realised that Udela was not looking at him, but now it was because she was embarrassed at what he was saying, not because she was shocked.

"Forget Lady Marlene and all the people like her," the Duke said firmly, "and that includes my brother and his appalling behaviour towards you."

He saw the expression of fear sweep over Udela's face as he mentioned Lord Julius.

"Have you ... have you ... heard from him?" she asked after a moment.

"He came to see me the afternoon before we left London," the Duke replied.

"Was he ... very angry that I ... escaped?"

"He was not aware at first to whom I was engaged, not having seen the *Gazette*. When he did know, it only added to his fury and his hatred of me. He wants to take my place and become the Duke of Oswestry, but there is nothing we can do to help him in that particular, so I suggest you forget his very existence. I promise you I will make quite certain he does not frighten you again."

"How can you be ... sure of that?" Udela asked.

The Duke knew she was thinking of what would happen to her when his need for a pretence engagement was over and she was on her own.

"We will discuss that later," he said. "While you are here with my grandmother and me, I promise you that you are as safe as if you were locked in a vault in the Bank of England, but very much more comfortable!"

Udela gave a little laugh, as he had meant her to do.

"Very, very much more comfortable!" she agreed. "I have never seen a more magnificent house, nor had my every wish supplied almost before I realised what I wanted."

"That is what I like you to feel," the Duke said, "and if my house was not run on greased wheels, I assure you I should blame myself and my own powers of organisation."

"You are very clever in that particular as well as in so many other things," Udela said.

He was glad to hear the admiration in her voice and see that it was back in her eyes.

"Tomorrow morning," he said, "now that you are no longer trying to hide from me, I suggest we ride together. I want to show you the parts of the Estate I loved best when I was a boy, and my favourite path through the woods, which as a child I was certain was full of fire-belching dragons!"

"And now you have grown up," Udela said in a soft voice, "you have . . . rescued the lady they were . . . menacing . . . but in London."

"There will be no more dragons," the Duke said firmly, "but only elves and nymphs, or whatever supernatural beings bring good luck to all those who see them."

As he spoke, he thought he was being unusually imaginative for a man who considered himself a cynic, but it was a reward in itself to see the smile which made Udela look even lovelier than she had ever done before.

* * *

Udela went into the Duchess's room to show her the new riding-habit which had arrived from London the previous day.

It was a habit to be worn in the summer and so

was of a light material, its colour echoing the blue
of her eyes.

Beneath the jacket trimmed with braid she wore
a thin muslin blouse fastening at her throat with a
bow, and there was a gauze veil from her high-
crowned hat which hung down her back and would,
she thought, float out behind her when she galloped.

The Duchess looked at her appraisingly.

"You look lovely, child," she said. "That habit is
certainly extremely becoming, and another should
be here in a day or so."

"I feel that is a needless extravagance," Udela
answered. "I can only wear one at a time."

"You will want to look different even when you
are riding," the Duchess said. "Think how bored
my grandson would become if you wore the same
gown night after night."

"I wonder if he would notice," Udela said, almost
as if she spoke to herself.

"Of course he would notice!" the Duchess replied
sharply. "Even if he does not compliment you as he
should, Udela, Randolph has always been partnered
by extremely attractive, well-dressed women, and
he considers their appearance a compliment to himself. I assure you that if you looked shabby or unattractive he would soon lose interest."

Udela wondered to herself if the Duke's interest
in her had anything to do with her appearance.

She had arrived at an opportune moment, she
realised now, to save him from Lady Marlene's demands that he should marry her, and his decision
to announce his engagement had nothing to do with
her personally.

Anyone who was fairly presentable would have
done, and it was, she thought to herself, only the
Duke's far-famed luck that she was pretty and

presentable enough for his relatives and everybody else to believe in all sincerity that he had fallen in love.

"What is worrying you?" the Duchess asked unexpectedly.

Udela did not reply and after a moment the Dowager went on:

"I noticed yesterday that you did not seem very happy. Surely you and Randolph have not quarrelled?"

There was a note of anxiety that was inescapable in the Duchess's tone, and Udela said quickly:

"No, Ma'am, there is nothing wrong . . . and we understand each other perfectly."

"That is all right then," the Duchess said with relief. "I could not bear, Udela, and this is the truth, that anything now should prevent your marriage."

Udela drew in her breath.

"If you only knew," the Duchess went on, "how I have prayed night after night, year and year, that Randolph would not only be married but find the happiness which I have always thought eluded him."

She gave Udela a little smile that was somehow very pathetic.

"You are too young to understand, dearest child, but a man who is always chasing women is not really happy. He thinks he is, but true happiness comes from being part of a family, from having a wife and children and facing the difficulties of the world together."

Udela drew in her breath.

"That is . . . what I would . . . like."

As she spoke, she knew that was what she had always wanted—a home of her own, to feel she belonged, and, more than anything else, to give her love to somebody who loved her in return.

"That is what you will have," the Duchess said, "but to make Randolph happy, you must always do what he wishes, at least ostensibly!"

She gave Udela a little smile as she said the last words, then explained:

"A woman who has a man in love with her can always get her own way. She does not have to say so, she merely has to make him think it is his way."

Udela gave a little laugh.

"I am sure that is what my mother did."

"It is a method used by all clever wives," the Duchess said, "and with Randolph it will be particularly necessary, because he has been spoilt! He likes to think that everything that happens is due to his own cleverness, but the fact that you will have a great deal to do with it is a secret you must keep to yourself."

"I understand," Udela said.

She bent and kissed the Duchess, saying as she did so:

"I must hurry or I shall keep him waiting."

"Enjoy yourself, and do not forget that you have both made me very, very happy."

"I will not . . . forget."

As Udela walked away from the Duchess's room she wondered how she and the Duke would ever be able to tell someone so kind as his grandmother that they were not to be married.

'It will hurt her and make her desperately unhappy,' Udela thought with consternation.

Then because it was so exciting to be riding with the Duke, she ran down the stairs, seeing, as she did so, that the horses were already outside the door and he was with them.

They galloped first through the Park, startling the deer clustered in the shade under the oak trees.

"You ride superbly!" the Duke said.

"Do you really think so, or are you just . . . saying it to be . . . kind?" Udela asked.

"I am telling you the truth."

"I am so glad . . . so very glad. It would please Papa more than anything else. But I have never before ridden such a fine horse as this one."

"I have a whole stable from which you can take your choice."

"You have everything," Udela said. "A stable full of magnificent horses, and Libraries filled with books, every one of which I would like to read."

She had been into the Library at Oswestry House on her way down to breakfast and she had found it the most impressive room she had ever seen, with a balcony running round the upper half of it.

She had also never imagined that one private person could own such a huge collection of volumes.

"You have certainly set yourself a formidable task," the Duke said with a laugh. "How long do you think that would take you?"

"A lifetime," Udela replied without thinking.

Then as it crossed her mind she knew it also crossed the Duke's that she would not be staying long enough to read even a small fraction of what the Library contained.

Because she was embarrassed, she touched her horse with her whip and rode ahead.

The Duke caught up with her as she saw there was a large wood ahead of them.

"This is the wood which you were telling me about?" she asked him.

"Yes," he replied. "There is a Ride through the middle of it which I think you will find very intriguing. I came here first on my pony when I could not have been more than five or six years old, and every time I return home, on the first or second day of my arrival I ride through the wood to where at the far end of it there is a pool in which, when I was a small boy, I was allowed to bathe."

"Not in the lake?" Udela asked.

She was thinking of the large lake which lay in front of the house and which in the early morning, with the mist rising from it, she had thought looked entrancing.

"That came later," the Duke answered, "when I was older, but the one in the wood had a magic for me that I have never forgotten."

Udela looked at him with a little smile.

When he talked to her like this, she thought he was very different from the frightening and cynical man she had first met in London.

They entered the wood and she could understand why he found it so attractive.

The Ride lay between rows of fir trees and was covered by grass and a fine moss that made their horses move almost silently.

The firs were very old and very high and it was like moving in a silent world where nothing could encroach, not even the troubles and difficulties that lay outside.

They rode in silence until as the Ride turned Udela saw on their right, high against the sky, the roof of what appeared to be a house.

She looked up at it in surprise, wondering why the Duke had not said that someone lived in the wood, when following the direction of her eyes he explained:

"That is the haunted house."

"Tell me about it," she pleaded.

"It is very old, and because it is haunted, or supposedly so, no one on the Estate will go near it. In fact it was burnt down over fifty years ago and is only a shell with part of the walls standing and a small portion of the roof. The rest was burnt or has crumbled away with age."

"Who built it, and why is it haunted?"

"It was built originally by one of my eccentric relations, who disliked the rest of the family and especially my grandfather who was the Duke at that time. He therefore built himself this house and lived, I believe, in great comfort with a number of servants to attend him."

"Then what happened?" Udela asked.

"He died and immediately the house was taken over by an even more eccentric relative, a cousin who was supposed locally to be a magician."

"And was he?"

"I personally think he was nothing of the kind. He was only interested in the supernatural, but because he was a recluse and wanted to see no one and speak to no one, he lived here alone with only one old servant to care for him."

"Go on!" Udela begged. "What happened?"

"Perhaps he was experimenting in some way or perhaps it was just an accident, but the house was set on fire and both my cousin and his servant were burnt to death."

"How terrible!"

"I am afraid nobody mourned him, but you can understand that locally, because they had been frightened of him in his lifetime, they were even more frightened of him dead. They say that he haunts the house, and there is no one, not even the most sensible game-keeper, forester, or villager, who will go near the house whether by day or by night."

Udela laughed.

"I understand how legends grow up. There was an old woman in my village who everybody said

was a witch simply because she talked to herself
and owned a black cat!"

"Simple people are very superstitious," the Duke
said. "And now I think we should go a little faster
because I want to show you my magic pool which
is still some way ahead."

"It is a very big wood."

"Very big," the Duke agreed. "I am always being pressed to cut down some of the trees, but I
like it as it is."

"So do I."

They rode on, then suddenly Udela saw something strange ahead of them on the path.

For a moment she could not think what it was.
Then as she drew nearer she saw it was a man.

He was lying spread out on the Ride as if he had
fallen forward.

It flashed through her mind that he might be
dead, and as she drew in her horse she said to the
Duke:

"What has happened to that man?"

"I will go and see," the Duke replied. "Hold my
bridle."

He gave it to her as he spoke and dismounted,
walking towards the man who looked to Udela as
if he was certainly unconscious.

His arms were stretched out in front of him and
his face was hidden.

The Duke went down beside him on one knee.
Then as he did so, suddenly two men from behind
the trees on each side of the Ride ran towards him.

Before he could move, they seized him by the
arms while at the same time the man who was lying
on the ground turned over and rose to his feet.

Udela was so astonished at what was happening
that she did not hear someone come up behind

her, and only as she was dragged roughly from the saddle did she give a cry of fear.

Before she could scream again a hand was put over her mouth. Then as she struggled, it was taken away only so that a handkerchief could replace it, gagging her as it was tied tightly behind her head.

It was then she realised that there were two men beside her, but when she would have looked at them, her hat was knocked from her head and a sack descended over her face and was pulled down over her shoulders.

She felt her gloves pulled from her hands and her wrists being tied fast by a rope, then her ankles.

Another rope was wound round her waist so that not only her wrists but the lower part of her arms were completely immobilised.

Then with a terror that seemed to pierce through her like a thousand knives she felt herself being lifted off the ground and was aware that two men were carrying her.

They started to move, and even through the confines of the thick sack which made it hard to breathe she could hear their feet crunching on twigs and what she thought were pine-needles.

That meant that they were carrying her through the wood, and she was sure of it when after a short while her head was tipped below her feet at an uncomfortable angle, and she knew that they were moving uphill.

She wondered frantically if the Duke was being carried in the same way, but if he was, she was not able to hear the sound of any other men moving. What made the situation even more frightening was that nobody spoke.

"Where are they taking me?" Udela asked and she ended with the prayer, "God, save me!"

She thought that once again Lord Julius was

determined to get her into his clutches and was carrying her away to some evil house as he had intended to do in the first place, and now there would be no escape.

The idea was so horrifying that she felt almost as if she must faint from sheer fear.

But because she was still conscious she could only go on praying frantically and fervently to God, to her mother, and to her father, to save her as she felt they had saved her before.

The men who carried her must have reached the top of the incline, for now her body was level and they paused for a moment before walking on, with the sound of their footsteps now quite different.

Then once again she was tipped up, but this time her head was above her feet and she knew she was being carried down a staircase of some sort.

Now for the first time she heard the footsteps not of two men but four.

She guessed that meant that the Duke was with her, and although Udela was horrified that he should also be a prisoner, it was still a relief to know that she was not alone.

She reasoned to herself that if it was Lord Julius who was carrying her away, he would do so in a carriage.

There might be one waiting somewhere, although they had not yet reached it, but for the moment at any rate she was near the Duke and near Oswestry House.

Surely there would be someone who would come to their rescue?

Suddenly and unexpectedly she was laid down roughly on the floor.

It was painful because her arms were tied behind her and she was turned a little sideways. At the same time, she felt the sack which had been over her head being dragged roughly away.

For a moment she thought she must have gone blind, for everything was dark.

Then she was aware that she was lying on a hard stone-paved floor which she could feel against her hands, while standing near her and towering above her were some men.

She thought there were three or four of them, but she could not be certain in the darkness.

Then suddenly there was a light and as she looked towards it she saw that it was a lantern carried by a man who was descending the stairs down which she must have been carried.

He came nearer, his footsteps ringing out on the paved floor, and by the light of the lantern she could just see his clothes, which were those of a gentleman.

Then as he came nearer she saw his face.

She felt herself wince, and if it had been possible she would have shrunk away into the very floor itself; for it was Lord Julius who was carrying the lantern!

Lord Julius, with an expression on his face which terrified her to the point where she wanted to scream.

Then as he looked first at her, then to her right, she saw what she had not noticed before. The Duke was lying a few feet from her, gagged and tied up as she was, his hands behind his back, a rope round his body and wound closely over his Hessian boots.

She knew it was impossible for him to move, but she could see that his smart, close-fitting coat was torn at the shoulders and the buttons had been ripped off, and she knew he must have put up a tremendous fight to prevent himself from being taken prisoner.

Lord Julius stood looking at his brother for some moments as if he enjoyed seeing him helpless, then he said:

"I suppose you know, dear Randolph, where I have brought you. And even you must admit that it is a very ingenious solution to my problem."

The way he spoke was so unpleasant and at the same time so triumphant that Udela felt he was as repulsive as a reptile.

"You know as well as I do that no one will come near the haunted house, and here in the cellars, my dear brother, you will rot and die!"

Lord Julius paused for a moment and glanced at Udela.

"And your fiancée, with whom our relations are so delighted, will die with you!"

There was an unpleasant twist to his lips as, still looking at Udela, he continued:

"It distresses me to think of that young and to me valuable body being caressed only by the worms, but it is a sacrifice I have to make."

He lifted the lantern a little higher as if to see the Duke more clearly as he gloated.

"You will die, Randolph, slowly and, I am afraid, painfully, but do not worry. I shall carry on the Dukedom in your absence and my son will inherit after I am dead, instead of yours, and the Westrys will not be forgotten."

He gave a laugh and it was a very unpleasant sound.

"I thought, knowing how proud you are of the Westry name, that you would not approve of one of us committing murder. So instead you will just rot away and there will be no one to tell the tale but the bats, the mice, and the foxes which enter a haunted house when no one else will."

He lifted the lantern still higher as he declaimed:

"I have won! I, Julius, the despised second son, for whom nobody ever had a kind word, have won!"

It was, Udela thought, the cry of a madman. Then he turned to the men who were listening and watching.

"Come away, fellows," he said. "Let us leave these wretches to their eternal rest! R.I.P. and good riddance! I will pay you well for your services, and that is the last money I shall spend of my own. Tomorrow I shall be in control of the Ducal funds."

He shouted the last two words and they seemed to echo and re-echo round the cellar.

Then as the men, who Udela could see were rough, unpleasant types, walked away towards the stairs as if they were pleased to go, Lord Julius hesitated.

"One thing I forgot, dear brother," he said. "The ring on your little finger with which every Duke of Oswestry seals his letters."

He walked to the Duke and, to Udela's horror, deliberately kicked him over on his side.

He put down the lantern he was carrying and, bending, pulled from the Duke's little finger the signet-ring which Udela had noticed before was the only jewellery he ever wore.

Lord Julius held it for a moment between his first finger and thumb before he put it on.

"A very valuable emerald, I have always been told."

He mouthed the words with unmistakable pleasure.

"But what is really valuable to me," he went on, "is the insignia on it. As the fifth Duke of Oswestry, I shall use it and use it frequently, and you can think of me doing so as you lie there and—die!"

He spat the last words at his brother, put the ring on his finger, and picked up the lantern.

The men had reached the bottom of the staircase and were standing waiting for him.

He walked towards them with a swagger and, passing ahead of them, climbed up the stone stairs.

The light dwindled and dwindled until finally it vanished.

Chapter Six

After Lord Julius had gone and the men had followed him up the stairs, for a moment Udela lay feeling it was hard to breathe.

She could not believe that it had all actually happened and was not part of some terrible nightmare from which she could not awake.

Then she realised that the gag across her mouth was hurting her almost intolerably and that the rope round her wrists was cutting into her flesh.

She was aware that there was a faint light coming not only from the direction of the stairs but also from the roof overhead.

She knew it was only a faint percolation of daylight through floors which had rotted, or perhaps from the entrance to the cellar where a door did not shut properly, but when she saw it she turned her head and could see indistinctly the Duke lying with his back to her.

It was then that an idea came to her and she thought it must be the recollection of some game she had played when she was a child.

With an effort she turned her body to the left so

that she had her back to the Duke. Then with difficulty and because at the same time it was painful, she managed to edge herself along the floor towards him.

It seemed to her to take a very long time, but finally her fingers touched his arms, and when she felt the cloth of his coat she slipped her body lower until the tips of her fingers touched his.

Instantly she felt him respond, and because she was touching him some of the terror, which had made her feel as if she wanted to scream frantically and go on screaming, seemed to vanish, and she felt she could think more clearly what she must do.

Because she had been so tightly bound it was hard to move her hands at all, but somehow by twisting her body as if it were a lever to propel her fingers, she found the knot which fastened the Duke's wrists.

The men had tied him with a coarse common rope which Udela knew would, if she could manage it, be easier to undo than one which was expensive and better-made.

Even so, the knot was tough, and although she pulled and pulled at it she feared that as her nails broke and her fingers began to ache, it would be impossible for her to loosen it.

Despairingly she realised that if she could not do so, they would die here on the stone floor of the haunted house, as Lord Julius intended.

The effort she had been making had made her very hot, and now to her delight she found that she could slip her mouth free of the handkerchief which gagged her.

"I can . . . speak!" she exclaimed in a voice which did not sound like her own, and added:

"I must get . . . you free . . . I must."

She had another idea, and, sliding farther down

the floor, she turned over and now her lips instead of her fingers found the knot.

She had always known that she had strong teeth.

In fact her father had teased her and said it was very unladylike to crack a nut with them, and her mother had reproved her over and over again for biting her thread with which she was sewing because it was quicker than finding a pair of scissors.

With her teeth Udela worked away at the rope and as she did so she prayed that she would be successful.

She thought of the vitriolic jealousy in Lord Julius's voice when he had jeered at his brother and the mad way in which he had shouted that he had won.

She could imagine how he would behave if he became, as he planned, the Duke of Oswestry.

She thought too of how it would hurt the Duchess to learn that she had lost the grandson she loved and that Lord Julius had taken his place.

"I must . . . save you . . . I must!" Udela said silently to the prostrate Duke.

Although he could not move, she had the feeling that he was willing her to succeed and she could almost feel the vibrations coming from him.

Then as her teeth pulled and pulled, suddenly and almost unexpectedly the rope came free.

For a moment she could only put her head down on the floor and breathe deeply because the effort had sapped her strength.

Then she realised that the Duke, aware of what was happening, was moving his hands and shaking his arms.

She wanted to help him but was too exhausted and could only listen to the struggle he was making beside her.

Then with a sigh of relief the Duke must have

removed his own gag, because he said in what sounded almost like his normal tone:

"Are you all right? Those devils have not hurt you?"

"No . . . I am . . . all right," Udela answered, but her voice sounded hoarse and strange.

It was a joy to be able to speak and to know that her lips, though they were stiff, could move.

The Duke ran his hands down her arms, then very gently turned her so that she had her back to him.

"Let me get your hands free," he said, "then we can take off the rest of the ropes."

He spoke calmly and kindly as he might have done to a frightened child, and she made an almost superhuman effort to control her feelings and to say:

"Lord Julius . . . kicked you . . . and I was . . . afraid he might have . . . injured you."

"I am bruised from the fight," the Duke replied, "but there are no bones broken, and all that matters, Udela, is that we should get home safely and as quickly as possible."

As he was speaking he was undoing the rope which had tied her hands together, and, having done so, he helped her to sit up so that he could unwind those which had confined her body.

He untied her ankles, then began to release himself.

Finally he rose to his feet and, holding out his hands to Udela, said:

"If you feel you can walk, I suggest that the sooner we get out of here, the better!"

Udela put her hands in his and managed to stand up.

The Duke put his arms round her shoulders and they walked together across the stone floor towards the stairs, guided by the dim light above them.

Only as they reached the steps did Udela say in a frightened whisper:

"You do not ... think those men will be ... waiting outside?"

"I think it would be very unlikely," the Duke replied. "They will get away as quickly as possible in whatever vehicle conveyed them here. But I imagine they will have taken our horses and therefore we will have to walk."

Udela wanted to say that she would walk a hundred miles if she could get back to the safety and security of Oswestry House. But she was afraid to speak, knowing that voices carried and that if there was a man on guard outside they might be attacked.

As if the Duke thought the same thing, he took his arm from her and walked up the steps ahead, very slowly pushing open the door which led from the cellar.

As Udela had thought, the wood of the door had cracked with age and the lock had broken.

Because Lord Julius had been so convinced that they would not be able to escape from their bonds and there was no chance of anyone coming to rescue them, he had not troubled to bar the door in any way but had just left it as it was.

The Duke looked about him cautiously, then stretched out his hand behind him as a signal to Udela to join him. She did so hurriedly, holding on to him as if he were a life-line.

"There appears to be no one about," the Duke said softly, his voice no louder than a whisper.

They walked outside, where after the dank chill of the cellar the air felt fresh, and Udela drew in several deep breaths before she said:

"Please ... let us hurry away."

"That is what I intend to do," the Duke said, "but it would be fool-hardy not to be cautious."

"Of . . . course," she answered, and her fingers tightened on his.

Drawing her by the hand, the Duke started to walk through the trees in front of the haunted house, moving downhill.

Udela was aware that he was going back to the Ride, and while she knew it would be easier walking, she would have preferred, however difficult it might be, to remain concealed amongst the firs.

But as the wood was very old and the trees had grown very large, it would in fact have taken them a long time to push their way through what had become an almost impenetrable forest.

She therefore resigned herself to letting the Duke have his own way, and they walked on down until some way below them Udela had her first glimpse of the Ride.

Then she gave a sudden gasp and pulled at the Duke's hand, bringing him to a standstill.

She did not speak—she was too terrified to do so.

Below them, lying on the Ride, there was a man!

It was almost as if they were re-enacting something which had happened before, and Udela felt with a sudden terror that this was another trap!

At any moment they might be recaptured and taken as prisoners back to the cellar from which they had escaped.

She looked about her wildly, thinking that perhaps they had a chance to run away.

Then she was aware that the Duke, standing very still, was staring at what they could see of the man lying on the Ride.

It was not easy to see him very clearly because he was partly obscured by the branches of the trees which lay between them and him.

After a moment the Duke said in a strange tone:
"Stay here! I am going down to investigate."

"No . . . no!" Udela whispered. "You cannot . . .
do that! It is a . . . trap! They are trying to . . .
trick you and are waiting to . . . pounce on you as
they did . . . before!"

She only whispered the words, but even so it was
a whisper frantic with fear, and she put out her
hands to hold on to the Duke.

"Please do . . . not go," she pleaded.

"It is all right," the Duke said quietly. "Stay
here! I promise you I will be careful, but I have to
see what has happened."

"No . . . no!"

"Trust me."

"You may be . . . killed! If Lord Julius is . . .
there, he will . . . kill you!"

"I do not think so," the Duke said. "Do as I tell
you, Udela, and wait here for me."

As he spoke, he moved her a few feet to the
right of where they were standing, and she found
herself sitting on the fallen trunk of a tree.

"Do not speak or move!" he ordered.

Then, while her hands tried to hold on to him,
he moved away from her and walked between the
fir-trees down towards the Ride.

Because she was quite certain that this was yet
another of Lord Julius's plans to destroy them,
Udela put her hands up to her face and covered
her eyes.

She knew she could not bear to see the Duke
captured or killed, as she was quite certain he
would be, and she told herself that if he was dead
she would want only to die too.

Before he reached the Ride, the Duke waited
behind a tree, looking round him in every direction
to make sure that Udela's fears were groundless.

He was sure in his own mind that anyone who could behave as his brother had done would move as quickly as possible from the scene of the crime.

He also knew that the type of men whom Lord Julius had employed were the roughest and most unscrupulous dregs from the underworld who would do anything for money but were in fact desperately afraid of being hanged or transported.

There were at least two or three charges on which they could incur one or the other of those penalties, and all they would want would be their money and to get back to London as quickly as possible.

The Duke reasoned that his brother would have brought them down in a brake or vehicle of some sort, which he would have left on the farm-track which lay on the other side of the wood.

Only Julius would have been aware that his brother, as was his usual habit, would have ridden in the wood as soon as he arrived home, and his plot had worked out according to plan, with the exception that he had not expected Udela to be so resourceful in untying their bonds.

The Duke was a very strong man but he had been powerless against three burly men who had taken him at a disadvantage.

He was aware too that while they could have laid him out with a blow from a heavy stick or just as easily knifed him, Julius in his madness had wanted him to die slowly and painfully of starvation.

The Duke looked once more up and down the Ride and across it, then stepped from behind the tree where he had concealed himself and walked towards the prostrate figure Udela had seen.

When he reached him he knew that what he had suspected was true and it was Julius who lay there.

He was dead. There was a blood-stained wound on his head where he had been struck with some heavy weapon and there was a knife in his chest just above his heart.

The blood from it had seeped all over his clothes but it was easy to see that his pockets had been rifled. What was more, and the Duke was sure this was the reason why he had been killed, the emerald signet-ring was gone from his little finger!

He remembered his brother's voice as he had gloated:

"A very valuable emerald, as I have always been told!"

The Duke thought he could imagine nothing more likely to be a temptation to the ruffians he had employed than the ring.

He stood for a moment looking down at the blood-stained body of his brother and wondered how it was possible that a man could have wasted and misused his life to the point where he became, for no reason except jealousy and hatred, a felon.

Then with a little sigh, knowing that there was nothing he could do, he started to walk back through the trees towards Udela.

As he neared her he was aware that she had her hands over her eyes and that her whole body was tense with fear.

His footsteps made no sound on the sandy ground, and as he reached her he thought that the faint shafts of sunlight percolating through the fir-trees, which turned her hair to gold, were very beautiful.

"Udela!" he called softly.

She gave a little cry and took her hands from her face to look up and see him standing in front of her.

It was then, without thinking, that she rose and flung herself against him.

"You are . . . safe! Thank God . . . you are safe!" she cried. "I thought they would . . . capture you!"

As she reached him his arms went around her and she burst into tears.

It was as if the relief swept away the control she had kept for so long and it was a tempest breaking.

"It is all right," the Duke said quietly, and he knew even as he spoke that she did not hear him.

"I thought . . . you would . . . die!" she sobbed. "I could not . . . bear it!"

"I am alive," the Duke said, "and so are you, Udela, so let us go home."

He thought for a moment that she had not heard him. Then slowly she raised her head from his shoulder to say a little incoherently:

"You are . . . sure it is . . . safe?"

Her eyes searched his as if to make certain that he was telling her the truth.

There were tears on her cheeks and her eyelashes were wet, and he thought as he looked down at her that she was lovelier in her distress than anyone he had ever seen.

"I promise you need no longer be afraid," he said.

As she continued to stare at him with her lips parted, he bent towards her and his mouth was on hers.

For a moment she could not believe it was happening.

Then as she felt his lips take possession of her, Udela knew that she loved him and this was why she had been so frantically afraid of losing him.

The Duke raised his head.

"Everything is all right," he said quietly, "and I

think we have both had enough dramatics for one day."

Then he was leading her through the trees, and because it was impossible to walk except in single-file, he went ahead, drawing her by the hand.

For a moment Udela was hardly aware where she was going or what she was doing.

She could think only of the wonder of the Duke's lips, and that he had kissed her was the most marvellous, perfect thing that had ever happened.

'I love him! I love him!' she thought to herself as her feet automatically did what was required of them.

Then she remembered that to the Duke, their engagement was only a pretence to avoid the outrageous demands of Lady Marlene.

When he had kissed her it had only been out of kindness and to reassure her that her fears were unnecessary.

'Whatever the reason,' Udela thought to herself, 'it is something I shall never forget, and no one will ever again make me feel that a kiss is a gift from God.'

They walked for quite a long time through the trees before the Duke turned down towards the Ride.

It was only then that Udela remembered the fallen man he had gone to investigate, and she realised that the reason they had walked so long through the trees was to avoid her seeing him.

She waited until they had actually reached the Ride before she asked:

"Was the . . . man you looked at . . . dead?"

"Yes," the Duke replied. "But we will talk about it later."

He started to walk rather quickly in the direction from which they had originally come, and after a second or two Udela said:

"I have a feeling ... although I may be wrong ... that it was ... Lord Julius."

"You are right," the Duke admitted. "It was my brother, and he had been murdered!"

Udela drew in her breath.

"Those men killed him, I imagine," the Duke went on, "for the emerald ring he took from me."

"It is ... horrible to think of ... their doing ... such a ... thing," Udela said in a low voice, "but I cannot feel ... sorry."

"Try not to think about it."

He was looking ahead and he gave a sudden exclamation:

"The horses!"

Udela looked too and saw that the horses they had been riding were on the Ride, with their heads down, quietly cropping the grass.

"We are lucky to be saved from the very long walk home," the Duke said with a smile.

He did not say so to Udela, but he thought that, having killed Julius, the robbers had fled panic-stricken with their ill-gotten gains and had not given a thought, as his brother would have done, to the value of the horses or the money which would have been easily obtainable for the silver bridles and expensive saddlery.

What mattered at the moment was that he and Udela had a quick and comfortable way to return to Oswestry House.

Only as he reached the horses and caught hold of the bridle of the one she had been riding did the Duke say with a note of concern in his voice:

"Are you feeling well enough to ride, or would you prefer I put you on the front of my saddle?"

It flashed through Udela's mind that if he did

so, she would be close to him and it would be very wonderful.

Then she thought it might make him uncomfortable and she answered quickly:

"I am quite all . . . right, only like you a little . . . bruised."

The Duke lifted her up onto the saddle, then swung himself onto his own horse, conscious as he did so that his hip hurt from where his brother had kicked him and that in his fight with the men when they had captured him he had strained a muscle in one of his arms.

But these were minor discomforts compared to the fact that he and Udela were free and that Julius was no longer there to menace them in future.

He was quite convinced now that he had been right when he had thought that his brother was mad. At the same time, it would have been difficult and unpleasant to try to prove it or even to persuade Julius to have any treatment.

Now he would not act the hypocrite, would not pretend to himself that the world was not a cleaner and better place without Julius in it.

As they rode without haste back into the Park and had the first glimpse of the great house ahead of them, the Duke said:

"I think our story, Udela, must be that when we were riding in the woods we met Julius, and while we were talking to him a number of rough men, obviously highway-robbers of some sort or another, set upon the three of us."

Udela was listening as he went on:

"They knocked me unconscious when I tried to fight them, killed Julius, and then escaped with everything we possessed. As we had no weapons, it was impossible for us to defend ourselves."

Udela did not speak for a moment. Then she asked:

"Will you tell your grandmother the . . . truth?"

"Perhaps," the Duke replied. "I will think about it, but I would not wish to upset her."

"I do not think it would upset her, except to think that you might have been killed. She loves you and she has often told me so."

"That makes me very fortunate," the Duke said with a smile. "But when we arrive back, remember that our stories of what has occurred must be identical."

"I wish to . . . say very . . . little," Udela answered.

She did not add that one reason for this was that she felt completely and utterly exhausted.

She knew it was more mental than physical, but now that it was all over, the horror of what had happened began to sweep over her and she felt as if it was impossible to stay in the saddle and to go on riding.

She thought the Duke would despise her for being so weak, and yet it seemed an interminable time before at last they reached the bridge over the lake and moved towards the great porticoed front of the house.

The grooms were waiting for them, obviously thinking it was strange that they had been riding for much longer than might have been expected.

When they saw the Duke's appearance and that Udela was not wearing her hat, their eyes were full of curiosity.

The Duke drew his horse to a standstill, but Udela, holding on to the front of the saddle, no longer had any control over her reins.

A groom went to the head of her horse, but when she should have been ready to dismount she was unable to move. The Duke took one glance at her pale face and came to her side.

Gently he lifted her down from the saddle, holding her in his arms.

She gave a little murmur and shut her eyes, and her head fell against his shoulder.

* * *

Udela awoke and saw the sun seeping through the sides of the curtains in her bedroom.

For a long time she lay looking at it, trying to remember where she was.

Then gradually, through what seemed like layers of sleep, her mind began to work and she remembered drinking something which had been held to her lips a long, long time ago.

'That is what made me sleep,' she thought, then recalled why she was in bed.

She knew that the Duke had carried her upstairs after they had been riding, because she had come back to consciousness as he took her into her bedroom to lay her down gently on the bed.

"You have been very brave," he said. "Do not worry about anything, just rest."

She had wanted to hold on to him, to keep him beside her, but somehow he had vanished as if into the mist and she had been only dimly aware of the Housekeeper and the maids undressing her.

Later there had been a strange man at her bedside and she thought it must be the Doctor.

She could not remember what he had said, she only knew that after he had gone she had slept and gone on sleeping.

When she awoke, she had drunk something sweet and pleasant which had made her sleep again.

Now she moved a little in the bed and thought that her wrists hurt and also her legs.

The ropes!

They had been very painful, but now they were gone and she was free. And Lord Julius was dead!

The thought of that was almost like a breath of fresh air galvanising her to life.

She wondered if she should ring her bell, and as she thought of it the door opened and the Housekeeper came to her bedside.

She looked at her for a moment, then as Udela's eyes turned towards her, she said:

"You're awake, Miss. I expect you'd like something to eat."

"How ... long have I been ... here?" Udela asked.

"For two days."

"Two days?" Udela cried in astonishment.

"Yes, Miss. The Doctor thought you should get over the shock and he gave you something which made you sleep."

"Two days!" Udela said almost to herself. "I suppose I should get up?"

"Certainly not, Miss!" the Housekeeper said sharply. "The Doctor's instructions and His Grace's are that you're to rest as long as possible and anyway until after tomorrow."

The Housekeeper went across the room to draw back the curtains, and after she had cogitated over what had been said, Udela asked:

"Why ... after ... tomorrow?"

"It's the Funeral, Miss, and His Grace has given instructions that no ladies should attend it. Very sensible, I think. It's better there should be only gentlemen present on such gloomy occasions."

The Housekeeper's words made Udela think of the Duchess.

"How is Her Grace?"

"Very upset by what has occurred, Miss, but

now that you're awake, I feel sure Her Grace'll be along to see you. She's been asking after you a dozen times a day. Deeply concerned, she's been!"

It was after Udela had washed and changed into a fresh nightgown, having had her hair brushed and having eaten what seemed to her to be a delicious meal, that the Housekeeper informed her:

"Her Grace's coming to see you, Miss."

Udela propped herself up against the pillows and unaccountably felt a little nervous.

But when the Duchess came into the room, the smile on her beautiful face and the kindness in her eyes made Udela hold out her hands impulsively.

"My dear, how are you?" the Duchess asked. "I am deeply distressed that you should have had such an unpleasant experience on your first visit to what will be your future home."

The maid had placed a comfortable chair beside the bed, and as the Duchess sat down in it she said, still holding Udela's hand in hers:

"Randolph has told me how brave you were. He is very proud of you!"

Udela felt herself blush.

"He was brave! He tried to fight three men at once!"

The Duchess gave a little cry.

"I cannot bear to think of it! How could such a terrible thing happen here in the country where we have always been so safe?"

She paused, then added:

"I cannot remember ever hearing of Highwaymen or even a robbery in these parts for years and years!"

There was nothing Udela could say and so she was silent. Then the Duchess said in a very different tone of voice:

"What is important is that you should not be worried about it or feel afraid."

"I am not . . . afraid now," Udela said, knowing that as Lord Julius was dead, that was the truth.

"Then you are as brave as Randolph said you were," the Duchess replied. "I feared that after anything so unpleasant you would wish to return immediately to London."

"No, of course not," Udela answered. "I would much rather be here in the country."

The Duchess smiled as if that was what she had wanted to hear.

"I hope Randolph feels the same," she said, "then we can all enjoy ourselves once the Funeral is over."

She looked at Udela as if she wondered if she would have any comment to make about Lord Julius's death, and when she did not speak, the Duchess went on:

"It will be very quiet, as quite rightly Randolph does not want a great deal of scandal and publicity about the way in which Julius was killed. Only our immediate relatives will be present and neither you nor I are to attend the Service."

"I am . . . glad," Udela said faintly.

"So am I," the Duchess agreed. "Now let us talk of more pleasant things."

She glanced towards the wardrobe.

"I do not know whether you have been told, but quite a large number of your new gowns have arrived, and as they look very beautiful I am longing to see you in them."

"Perhaps I can get up tomorrow evening," Udela suggested, then thought that perhaps it would be too soon after the Funeral.

"A very good idea!" the Duchess approved.

"Everyone will have left, and you and I and Randolph will dine alone."

She smiled at Udela in an almost conspiratorial fashion and added:

"We must cheer him up. There is one piece of good news for him in the newspapers this morning, although I do not like to ask if he has seen it."

"What is that?" Udela asked.

"A very tiresome friend of his, a woman of whom I did not approve and did not like and who ran after him in an outrageous fashion, has been married."

In a voice that did not sound like her own Udela asked:

"W-who is . . . that?"

"You may not have heard of her," the Duchess replied, "although she is a great beauty. Her name is Lady Marlene Kelston, and she has married a man who I think is well suited to her, Lord Humberton. He is old and in my opinion unpleasant, but very, very rich!"

Udela shut her eyes.

With a note of concern in her voice, the Duchess said quickly:

"I must not tire you, dearest child, by talking any more. I shall leave you to sleep."

She rose to her feet and bent over to kiss Udela on the cheek.

"Sleep well, my dear. It is so wonderful to me to know how happy you and Randolph will be together."

The Duchess left the room and Udela did not move until she heard the door close behind her.

Then she turned on her side and buried her face in the pillow.

She knew what the Duchess's information about Lady Marlene meant!

Now, just as she was no longer menaced by Lord Julius, so the Duke was no longer menaced by Lady Marlene. He was free and there was no reason for their pretence engagement to continue.

"He will send me away," Udela told herself. "He will give me the thousand pounds he promised me and he will never think of me again."

As she thought, she remembered the moment he had kissed her in the wood. It had been the most marvellous thing that had ever happened to her in her whole life and something she vowed she would never forget.

But she was well aware that it was just an action of kindness from a man who was trying to protect her from her own fear.

Now he would have no further use for her, and as he had said so clearly in the contract he had drawn up and made her sign, she must leave "immediately and without complaint."

The words seemed to echo and re-echo in Udela's mind, and yet there was nothing she could do about them except leave as she had promised she would do.

Slowly the tears that filled her eyes began to run down her cheeks, then despairingly with a sob that seemed to come from the very depths of her soul, she said to herself over and over again:

"I love him! I love him!"

Chapter Seven

When the time came for Udela to rise and begin dressing for dinner, she wanted to say that she would rather stay in bed, that she felt too ill to go downstairs.

But she knew that was only putting off the inevitable, and she had to make the effort.

The maid who was attending to her only wished to talk about the Funeral.

"Ever so quiet, it was, Miss," she said, "but the flowers were beautiful! The gardeners were a-working all yesterday and the coffin looked a picture!"

Udela wanted to shudder even at the thought of Lord Julius, but she forced herself to murmur some conventional remarks and the maid did not realise that anything was wrong.

She learnt, however, that the Duchess was not feeling well and was what the maid called "resting."

Udela knew that even though she had not been fond of her grandson Julius, it was still hurtful to know that his life, bad though it was, had come to an end.

He was young and could have done so much
with his opportunities, but he had missed everything, even the affection he might have had from
his relatives.

However, it was difficult for Udela to think of
anything but herself.

After a night of misery, knowing that she was
crying for the moon and unable to stop herself
from doing so, she had tried to face the day sensibly.

"I have been lucky, very lucky, to have known
anyone as . . . wonderful as the Duke . . . even for
a . . . short time," she told herself.

She could not help wondering, since her life
would never be the same without him, if it would
have been better to have remained in ignorance of
how glorious love could be.

But she could not change fate.

When she was dressed in one of the lovely gowns
the Duke had given her, she looked at her reflection and thought she must make every effort to
enjoy this last dinner with him—the last hours, the
last minutes, the last seconds.

They would all become part of her memories,
and when she had left Oswestry House and was
living far away she would be able to picture him
in his own surroundings, hear his voice speaking,
see his handsome face at the end of the table.

"I love . . . him! I love . . . him!" she cried in her
heart, and she knew how horrified he would be if
he could hear her.

He had certainly not deceived her in any way
but had made it clear exactly what he required
and what he would pay for her services.

Udela could see all too clearly the words written
in his strong upright handwriting:

. . . when the time comes, leave immediately,
without complaint . . .

"I will never complain, and he must not guess
that I wish to do so," she murmured to herself.

She admonished herself even as her mother
might have done to behave like a lady, while her
father would have expected her to be sporting
about it.

Everything the Duke had done was fair and
above-board, and she knew that her father would
be deeply ashamed of her if at the last moment
she cheated over her part of the bargain.

She could not help thinking miserably that if
only Lady Marlene had not got married so quickly
and Lord Julius had not acted so speedily to rid
himself of his brother, she might have been able
to stay longer with the Duke.

She could also have worn more of the lovely
gowns which hung in the wardrobe, many of which
she had not even had time to examine since they
had arrived from London.

But that was "complaining" and what she had to
do was to say good-bye with a smile and to be
grateful that she had been privileged as few young
women in her circumstances were likely to be.

"You look ever so lovely in that gown, Miss,"
the maid was saying.

She made Udela remember that time was passing.

"Is Her Grace coming down to dinner?" she enquired.

"Oh, no, Miss! Her Grace has intimated that she
doesn't wish to be disturbed."

It was wrong, Udela knew, but she felt her heart
lift and beat faster.

At least she would have the Duke to herself for the last night.

Taking a quick look at her reflection in the mirror, she rubbed her cheeks so that they would not look so pale, then went down the Grand Staircase, resisting an impulse to run so that she could reach the Salon more quickly.

He was waiting for her and as she walked towards him he smiled and she felt as though the sun had come out.

"You are rested, I hope, Udela?" he said quietly.

"I am ... perfectly all ... right," she answered.

"It is always wise to take time to get over a shock."

She felt somehow as if they were making conversation when there were so many other things they might say.

He handed her a glass of champagne and as she took it from him she had the feeling that his eyes were looking at her penetratingly.

She thought that he was looking to see if she was telling him the truth and was really in good health after the ordeal through which she had passed.

Because she thought it would seem tiresome if she was nervous and making a fuss over what had occurred, she said:

"I have not seen your grandmother today, but I can understand that she did not wish for visitors."

"Grandmama has been magnificent about everything," the Duke said, "but, needless to say, anything so unnecessarily dramatic is upsetting at her age."

"Yes ... of course," Udela agreed.

Dinner was announced, and when the Duke offered her his arm, Udela felt herself quiver even though her fingers were lying very lightly on his arm.

Now that his signet-ring was gone, she noticed he wore no other jewellery, and she wondered if he missed the ring and if he was taking steps to recover it.

It would not be difficult to notify the "fences" or the places where thieves sold their stolen goods. This need not involve capturing the men who had killed Lord Julius, which she felt certain the Duke would not wish to do.

'Everything that happened must be forgotten,' she thought.

Once she had gone, there would be nothing left to remind the Duke of what for him must have been a particularly horrifying experience because one of his own flesh and blood was involved.

After they had started dinner, Udela realised that the Duke was making every effort to amuse and interest her.

He told her of his travels abroad and recounted fascinating stories about his family, the treasures in the house, and his other possessions in different parts of England.

She listened not only with interest but knowing that when she was no longer with him this would be something to remember.

It was not only what he said, but all the time she was deeply conscious of how elegant he looked as he sat at the top of the table.

It was as if everything in the room was centred round him and was there only as a perfect background for his vibrant personality.

It flashed through Udela's mind that they were both of them acting a part in a play which had a very small cast and a very small audience—themselves.

'Tomorrow the play will be over,' she thought, and felt her spirits fall.

For the moment, in her exquisite white gown, with the flowers in her hair and her skin glowing white in the flicker of the candles, she fitted to perfection the part she had to play.

And what could the Duke be but the leading man, the hero, not only to her but to any other woman he was with?

The dinner came to an end and Udela found herself dreading the moment when she must leave the table and walk back to the Salon.

But the moment came and she felt almost as if every step she made on the soft carpet whispered: "This is the last time ... the last time ..."

She would have returned to the Salon, but the Duke said:

"I thought we might sit in the Library tonight. I have something to give you."

As he spoke, she knew, as if it were a death-knell to her happiness, what that something was: the thousand pounds he had promised her and which he would doubtless hand her in the form of a cheque.

She wished that she could refuse and tell him, as she had done before, that it was too much. Then she knew it would only annoy him.

Because the contract between them had been timeless, three days, three months, three years, he would not change the bargain he had made, and to argue about it would be a waste of words.

At night in the glow of the candles, the Library looked different, Udela thought, from the way it looked in the daytime with the sunlight pouring in from the windows.

The curtains were drawn over all of them except one which opened out onto the terrace.

Because she thought she could not bear to look at the beauty of the sunset, she deliberately sat down in a chair with her back to it and waited for the Duke to speak.

"I have something to tell you, Udela . . ." he began.

He was standing, as she had expected, with his back to the fireplace, and even as he spoke she knew what he was about to say.

Because she could not bear to hear it a second time, she said quickly:

"If it is about . . . Lady Marlene, Her Grace has already . . . told me that she has . . . married."

"So you know! And she will no longer pester me with her lies."

"Yes . . . I . . . know."

There was silence. Then, as if Udela would force him to say the words she dreaded, she said quickly:

"I understand . . . that there is no need . . . for us to keep up our . . . pretence engagement . . . any longer . . . and I will . . . leave in the morning."

"Where will you go?" the Duke enquired.

Udela made a helpless little gesture before she said:

"I will . . . find somewhere."

"You do not intend to live alone?"

She was just about to say that she would not be alone if she rented a cottage in Little Storten, then she remembered that Lord Eldridge was at the big house and she had no wish to meet him.

He would know what Lord Julius had intended doing with her, and she had a horrifying feeling that it might influence his behaviour towards her, and she could not face the humiliation of it.

The Duke was waiting for her answer and after a moment she said:

"I will . . . think of . . . something."

"Surely that is an unsatisfactory way of planning your future?" the Duke observed.

"There is no need for ... Your Grace to ... worry about me," Udela answered. "You have been ... so kind ... so very kind ... and I feel ... embarrassed about the money you have spent on so many ... gowns ... most of which I have ... not even ... worn."

"You looked very lovely in those I have seen."

She glanced at him, surprised at the compliment.

Then she told herself that he was being kind and it was the sort of flattering thing a man in his position would say automatically to any woman he was with.

"I was wondering," he went on, "if you know of anyone whom you would like to talk to about your future plans?"

The Duke waited for her answer and Udela said quickly:

"N-not your grandmother ... and please do not think me ... impertinent ... but could you ... break it to her ... very gently, that we are not ... to be m-married?"

"You think it will upset her?"

"I know it will. She has been so happy ... so very happy about your ... engagement, and I know when she learns it is ... broken, it will give her deep distress."

Udela spoke in an agitated way simply because she was well aware that the Duchess would in fact be desperately unhappy to know that once again her hopes regarding her grandson were dashed to the ground.

Also, she had been so kind and so understanding in every way that although it seemed presumptuous, Udela knew she loved the Duchess as much as, if not more than, she would have loved her own grandmother.

"So you think my grandmother will be upset?" the Duke asked.

"I know she will be, and that is why I . . . beg of you not to give her a . . . shock by announcing . . . abruptly that everything . . . between us is over."

She thought for a moment, then she said:

"Perhaps you could say I have gone away for a little while to visit one of my own relatives . . . then when I do not return . . . perhaps it would be b-best to say . . . I had . . . died."

"Died?" the Duke questioned.

"It would be better . . . better for you."

"In what way?"

Udela chose her words with difficulty.

"I . . . I think . . . Her Grace feels that as your . . . love-affairs in the . . . p-past have lasted such a short . . . time . . . it is . . . usually your fault . . . and not that of the . . . l-lady in question."

She paused for a moment, then added:

"Of course . . . where Lady Marlene was . . . concerned, it was different because your grandmother did not . . . like her . . . and was glad . . . very glad when you were no longer . . . interested in her."

The Duke did not speak, and because she was nervous of what she had said, after glancing up at him Udela added quickly:

"Please . . . forgive me if I have . . . spoken of things which are not my . . . business . . . but I cannot bear your grandmother to be unhappy."

"Why should you feel that about someone you have only just met?" the Duke asked.

"One does not have to know someone for a long time either to love . . . or to hate them," Udela replied. "Where love is concerned, it can happen like a flash of lightning... and has... nothing to do with ... time."

She spoke with a little throb in her voice because she was thinking that her love for the Duke was the same as if she had known him for a thousand years.

She loved him and he filled her whole world, and when he would no longer be there, there would be only a vast emptiness.

"It seems strange that you should be so knowledgeable on the subject of love," the Duke said after a moment. "When we talked of it previously, you said that you were ignorant of that elusive emotion."

"I do not remember, Your Grace, ever speaking about real love," Udela replied, "only the sort which is... cheapened and degraded by being... sold in some way or ... another."

"But now I think you are talking of a very different type of love," the Duke said, "the love which comes from the heart. Am I right?"

"Y-yes."

"I should be interested to know your views."

Udela thought that would not only be a mistake but might be far too revealing.

How could she talk to the Duke about the feelings that seemed almost to choke her with their intensity, without his becoming aware that her whole being reached out towards him?

Because she felt agitated, she rose from the chair and walked towards the window.

As she had anticipated, the sun behind the trees in the Park was even lovelier than it had been on any other night.

The gold and crimson of it was reflected on the lake, and the sky above glowed with a translucence that made the whole scene enchanted and mysterious.

'I must remember it, I must remember it all,'

Udela thought to herself. 'It is the . . . last time I shall ever see . . . anything so lovely.'

"What are you thinking?" the Duke asked behind her.

"That I . . . I . . . did not know such beauty . . . existed."

"I have a feeling," the Duke said very quietly, "that you are saying good-bye to it."

He understood, and because there was something in his voice that vibrated within her, Udela felt the tears come into her eyes.

She *was* saying good-bye, but the real loveliness which would go from her life was in the hands of the man standing beside her; the man who had taken her heart and made it his.

"I suppose," the Duke said, "there are a great many conventional things I should say, and which we have not yet mentioned this evening."

Udela was still, but she did not turn round.

"First, I should thank you," he said, "for saving both our lives. I would not have believed that anyone could have been as clever as you were in undoing those ropes and that you found a way to do so which I admit I would not have thought of myself."

"I do not . . . want to be . . . thanked, Your Grace," Udela said. "I was . . . only so afraid that you might . . . die in such a . . . cruel and unnecessary manner."

"That *I* might die?" the Duke questioned. "What about yourself?"

"I am of . . . no importance in the world . . . but you are."

"You cannot expect me to believe that you are speaking seriously."

It flashed through Udela's mind that it would not have been so hard to die with the Duke dying with her, but it would be far harder to live without him.

Because she was afraid of what she might say, she merely went on staring at the sunset, aware that because there were tears in her eyes, the view was no longer clear.

"You were amazingly brave," the Duke said. "In fact I cannot imagine any other woman of my acquaintance who would have behaved not only with such courage but also with such self-control."

He was silent for a moment, then he added:

"The only time you seemed to break down a little was when you pleaded with me not to incur any further danger by going down onto the Ride to look at the man who lay there."

Udela could not speak, it was impossible to do so, and the Duke said, still in that quiet, calm voice:

"I wonder if you were really thinking of me."

"Of course I was!" Udela said quickly, without thinking. "It was brave . . . but fool-hardy . . . it could have been another trap . . . and you would not have been able to . . . escape for a . . . second time."

"When you found it was nothing of the sort," the Duke said, "and I came back to you, you seemed very glad to see me."

"I was . . . glad!" Udela murmured, barely above a whisper.

Then she remembered how the Duke had kissed her, and she felt again that sudden wonder and rapture which had swept through her at the touch of his lips.

Now the tears blinded her and she told herself it was because she was weak and still suffering from the shock.

She wanted to wipe her eyes, but she was afraid

that if she did so, the Duke would know she was crying.

"There is something I want to ask you," he said, "but it is rather difficult to talk to the back of your head."

Because of the tears on her cheeks Udela dared not turn round, nor for the moment was she capable of saying anything.

She could only feel an agony that grew and grew until she could think of nothing except that this was the last time she would hear him talking to her, the last time they would be near to each other.

He would thank her, and if she had any dignity, any pride, she would say good-bye as he expected her to do.

"Come here, Udela!"

Because there was a command in his voice that Udela dared not disobey, she pulled the tiny, lace-edged handkerchief from beneath one of her puff sleeves where she had tucked it away and wiped her tears.

Lifting her chin in an effort to appear proud and unconcerned, she turned and walked slowly back towards the Duke, thinking as she did so that he seemed larger and more overpowering than he had even a moment or so before.

Could any man be more handsome? She should in fact be eternally grateful that she had been able to save anyone so magnificent rather than die with him ignominiously.

He made no effort to move towards her, and when she reached his side he stood looking down at her for a long moment before he asked:

"Why are you crying?"

She thought it was such a foolish question that there was no point in answering it.

Instead she said:

"If you will . . . arrange it, I will leave first . . . thing in the . . . morning . . . before your grandmother is . . . awake."

"I imagine at that time I shall be riding," the Duke said, "so perhaps we should say good-bye now."

Udela drew in her breath and was very still. Then, almost as though someone spoke for her and it was not her own voice, she said in a whisper which he could barely hear:

"Before I go . . . can I . . . ask you . . . for something?"

She thought he was surprised at her question, and after a second he replied:

"Of course. What do you want?"

Again the voice that spoke was not her own.

"Would you . . . kiss me . . . just once . . . more . . . so that I will have . . . something to remember?"

She had said it! It had seemed impossible but she had said it!

She tried to look up at him but failed, and although her face was lifted to his her eyes were closed, because she was afraid to see the expression on his face.

For one anguished moment she thought he was about to refuse, then she felt his arms go round her and he pulled her against him, and his lips were on hers.

She knew then that this was what she had longed for and prayed for, not only since the moment he had first kissed her but almost since she had first known him.

There was not only the rapture and the wonder that he had given her when he had kissed her in the wood, but it was part of the beauty of the sunset, the glory of the sky, and the shimmering silver of the lake.

It was everything that was beautiful, including the house itself, and most of all it was the love she had felt growing within her until her whole being reached out towards him and there was nothing but him.

His lips became more possessive, more demanding, and he held her closer still until he gave her the moon and the stars and the whole world and there was nothing left to ask for because he had made it hers.

'This is love,' she thought, 'the love that I have sought but thought I would never find.'

She pressed herself nearer to him, praying that she could die because it would be impossible for her to know such happiness again.

Then, when she felt that time stood still, the Duke raised his head.

"Is that what you wanted?" he asked.

She looked up at him, bewildered at the very rapture and wonder of her feelings.

"I . . . want . . . to die," she murmured incoherently.

She hoped he had not heard what she said because it was a complaint.

Knowing she was about to cry, she freed herself from his arms and moved towards the door.

Her one idea was to go away. He had done what she had asked. Now she must fulfil her part of the bargain and leave him.

It seemed a very long way to the door, and her tears were falling quicker and quicker, but somehow she reached it.

Only as she actually touched the handle did she hear the Duke say:

"You have forgotten something, Udela."

She could not move, could not see, but he said insistently:

"I want you to have this."

Bending her head so that he should not see her face, she turned round and moved slowly towards him.

He must have met her halfway, because through her tears she suddenly saw his hand in front of her eyes and he was holding an envelope.

"This is for you."

She took it automatically, knowing what it contained.

When she would have turned away again, he said:

"I want you to look inside it."

She thought he wished her to check that it was the thousand pounds he had promised her.

"That . . . is . . . unnecessary."

"Open it, Udela!"

She felt she must obey him, and because she was holding a tight control on herself so as not to break down completely and fall sobbing at his feet, she did as she was told.

Somehow she had lost her handkerchief, but she wiped the tears from her eyes with the back of her first finger.

Then with hands that shook she opened the envelope which the Duke had given her.

She knew what she expected to find, and yet, because he was waiting beside her, she forced herself to look at what was in it, hoping frantically that it was not more money than he had already promised to give her, and wondering, if it was, how she could refuse to take it.

Then she saw that written on the paper were only three words. They were clear and firm and in

his strong upright handwriting which she had seen
only once before.

Udela thought that her eyes, blurred by tears,
were distorting what he had written, but still they
were there—just three words!

"I love you!"

She gave a little gasp, then the Duke's arms
were round her.

As she hid her face against him, he said very
quietly:

"Did you really think we could say good-bye to
each other, my darling?"

"It . . . cannot be . . . true!"

"It is true," he said. "It has been true for a very
long time. But I was afraid to tell you so."

"W-why?"

"Because I was not sure that you loved me, and
I could not bear to be tricked and deceived again."

"How could you imagine . . . I would . . . deceive
you?" Udela tried to ask.

But it was impossible to speak and almost impossible to think. All she knew was that the Duke's
arms were round her and her heart was singing
wildly and deafeningly because he had said that
he loved her!

The Duke put his fingers under her chin and
turned her face up to his.

"Look at me, my precious!"

Her eyes were shining even though her eye-
lashes were still wet.

"Now tell me," he said very gently, "what you
feel about me."

"I . . . love you," Udela said. "You know . . . I
love you . . . but how could I ever have . . . imagined that you would love . . . me?"

"I thought you loved me," the Duke replied,
"when I kissed you in the wood. But I told myself

I might have been mistaken and you only wanted my title and my money as so many other women have done in the past."

"How could you . . . think . . . such things?" Udela whispered.

"I thought them, but I did not really believe them," the Duke replied. "I was just protecting myself from being hurt."

"You . . . know I would . . . never hurt . . . you."

"I know that now," he said, "and my instinct told me when you were untying the ropes round my hands so cleverly that you were thinking more about me than yourself."

"I was . . . desperately . . . afraid that you . . . might . . . die!"

"My lovely one, you are so very, very different from anyone I have known before," the Duke said.

Then his lips found Udela's and he kissed her until the world swam dizzily round her and she thought she had in fact died and was in Heaven.

It seemed a very long time later that he drew her to the sofa and they sat down, his arms still about her.

"How soon will you marry me, my darling?"

She looked up at him, her eyes seeking his.

"You are . . . quite sure that I . . . ought to marry you? You are so grand . . . and I shall always be . . . afraid that when you . . . know me well . . . you will be disappointed."

"All my life I have known that you existed somewhere in the world," the Duke replied, "if only I could find you. Then, when I was so often disillusioned, I believed that it was impossible."

"Why were you so disillusioned?"

When he hesitated, she said quickly:

"You need not tell me if you do not wish to."

"I am hesitating, my precious," he replied, "because now that I have you, it all seems unimportant and indeed rather foolish."

"Tell . . . me."

"It is such an ordinary story that I am rather ashamed," he replied. "I fell in love when I was very young and idealistic with a beautiful girl who was a year younger than I was."

Udela felt a little dart of jealousy run through her, but she said nothing and the Duke went on:

"As she was eminently suitable in every way, our marriage was agreed between our parents, but we were told to wait until I was twenty-one."

"What . . . happened?"

"The girl I believed loved me as much as I loved her found somebody more important."

Udela thought that must have been impossible, until the Duke, as if he knew what she was thinking, explained:

"My rival was the reigning Prince of a German Principality—a small one, but nevertheless he was a Prince!"

"So she . . . broke off the . . . engagement."

"She told me that while she loved me, she wanted to be a Princess. It was as simple as that."

Udela did not speak and the Duke said:

"In fact, as you would put it, she sold her love for a Crown."

Udela put her arms round his neck as if she would protect him.

"How can I . . . ever make you . . . understand," she said, "that I would love you if you were as . . . poor as I am and if you were of no . . . importance whatsoever?"

Then with a little sob she added:

"I think in a way I would prefer that, because I could then . . . look after you and you would know that my love . . . rests not on anything you . . . possess or anything you could give me, but only because . . . you are . . . you."

The Duke held her so tightly that she could barely breathe.

"I know that already, my precious one," he said, "and when we were prisoners in that ghastly cellar, I thought that if I had to die I was glad to die with someone I loved."

"I thought . . . the same," Udela whispered, "but because I loved you so . . . overwhelmingly, I had to be sure you . . . lived, even though I could have no . . . part in your life."

"I love you!" the Duke said. "And I am going to spend my life making you realise the breadth, height, and depth of my love, my beautiful one. What is more, I swear I shall never let you be afraid again. The dragons have all gone, Udela, and never again will I let you be afraid or unhappy."

He kissed her eyes before he said:

"There will be no more terror, no more fear, and, my dearest heart, I want you to smile, I want to hear your laughter, and I want to be very, very sure that you love me as much as I love you."

"I do love you!" Udela said. "I love you until you are part of every breath I draw . . . every thought I have . . . every dream I . . . dream."

She spoke a little shyly and the Duke asked:

"You have dreamt of me, my adorable, precious little love?"

"Every night," Udela whispered, "and the last two nights when I have been awake in the darkness I have . . . pretended that you were . . . kissing me."

Her voice was very hesitant and very shy, and

once again the Duke turned her face up to his and looked down at her to say:

"There will be no need for any further pretences either that I am kissing you or that we are engaged. We will be married immediately and we will go abroad for our honeymoon so that no one will know."

"That would be . . . wonderful!"

"I have been thinking," the Duke went on with a smile on his lips, "that as Grandmama will be so delighted about our marriage, we can leave her to make the correct excuses so that people will forgive us for doing them out of a grand wedding."

"I only . . . want to be with . . . you."

"That is what I intended to say," the Duke answered. "We think alike on this, my darling, so that is one argument we need not have."

"I will never . . . argue with you . . . again."

"I am sure you will," the Duke answered, "but only about things that do not matter. What really matters, my darling, is that I have found the person who loves me for myself, and you have given me your heart and I think too your soul."

"You know . . . that is . . . true."

"And they are so precious, my wonderful one," the Duke said, "that no money, no title, could buy them."

"That is what I am . . . trying to make you . . . understand," Udela cried, "that without your love the whole world is . . . empty and dark, and I would rather . . . die than go on living."

"You will live," the Duke answered, "because I want you and because, my darling, we have so much love for each other that it will take a century of time to express it."

He was kissing her again, kissing her until Udela

felt he carried her up towards the stars that were now shining in the sky outside.

There were stars too shining in their hearts, in their minds, and in their souls; the stars of real love, which all men seek and some are privileged to find.

ABOUT THE AUTHOR

BARBARA CARTLAND, the world's most famous romantic novelist, who is also an historian, playwright, lecturer, political speaker and television personality, has now written over 200 books.

She has also had many historical works published and has written four autobiographies as well as the biographies of her mother and that of her brother Ronald Cartland, who was the first Member of Parliament to be killed in the last war. This book has a preface by Sir Winston Churchill.

Barbara Cartland has sold 100 million books over the world, more than half of these in the U.S.A. She broke the world record in 1975 by writing twenty books, and her own record in 1976 with twenty-one. In addition, her album of love songs has just been published, sung with the Royal Philharmonic Orchestra.

In private life, Barbara Cartland, who is a Dame of the Order of St. John of Jerusalem, has fought for better conditions and salaries for Midwives and Nurses. As President of the Royal College of Midwives (Hertfordshire Branch), she has been invested with the first Badge of Office ever given in Great Britain which was subscribed to by the Midwives themselves. She has also championed the cause for old people and founded the first Romany Gypsy Camp in the world.

Barbara Cartland is deeply interested in Vitamin Therapy and is President of the British National Association for Health.